INSIGHT PUBLICA

Kozhikode, Kerala, India 673011
www.insightpublica.com
e-mail: insightpublica@gmail.com
Voice of Women in Short Stories
India and Russia
(English)
JIMLY P.
First Edition: December 2019
This Edition: October 2021

ISBN 978-93-89804-05-8

VOICE OF WOMEN IN SHORT STORIES
India and Russia

JIMLY P.

Born at Ramanattukara in Kozhikode district. Father: P.Sudhakaran. Mother: M.K. Premalatha. Education: M.A in Comparative Literature (Calicut University), M.Phil in Comparative Literature (Calicut University), Ph.D in Comparative Literature. (Calicut University).

Husband: Nidheesh.A.

Children: Harigovind, Devalakshmi, Devanarayan.

Address: "Aswathy", Vaidyarangadi (P.O),
Ramanattukara, Kozhikode.

Jimly P.

CONTENTS

Preface

Women's writing in the present world have made a deep impact on the social and cultural ambience. Women's literature emerges out to be an outcry of a group of people who have remained suppressed, disregarded and abandoned under patriarchy and vested political groups.

In the present century one of the major topics for discussion among us is 'women and their problems'. In every corner of the world, women are facing problems as wife, lover, mother and daughter. In every field she has to face many problems. Almost all literary creations of the world narrate these problems. The postmodern era has witnessed a spurt in women's creative writing as well as in feminist literary criticism uncovering the ideology of patriarchal society in works of art.

The present work extensively dealt with the theme of man-woman relationship and parent-child relationship which have a great historical, sociological and cultural significance. The study proposes to critically examine and compare the treatment of the theme of familial relationship in the selected fictions of Natalya Baranskaya and Kamala Das. The two women writers Natalya Baranskaya and Kamala Das through their works are portraying woman's experiences of locations, cultures, language and ethos.

This book provides a mirror image of the changing roles of the different familial relationship depicted in the selected short fictions of Natalya Baranskaya and Kamala Das. It reveals that a human relationship is passing through a conflict in roles and values. This is owing to the swift changing taking place in our society in the relationship between man and woman, within family and outside home. Apart from sociological, historical and feministic involvements the subject is interesting in itself and it is unveiling of images of familial relationship in some of the contemporary fictions.

1
SHORT STORY AS A LITERARY FORM

Short story as a literary genre has a unique position in the world of literature. The 'shortness' itself makes it more popular in the society where the life is hectic and man is hard-pressed for time. In the fast moving society people prefer to complete each task within the limited available time. Such a social situation has given rise to the popularity of short story as one can satisfy one's literary urge within the limits of time at his or her disposal.

Short story as a kind of prose fiction, grew up apart from the novel, gained its unique position and attained recognition as a separate form of literature. Though immensely popular in modern times, the short story is not a modern product. It has been popular in every age and in every country. From times immemorial, people, old and young have always liked to be entertained and the short story has been their most popular entertainment. The earliest forms of the short story were the tales of adventure, dealing with the deeds of valour or of chivalry of some popular hero. Every country has got its own legends and mythology, and tales, from them or their modifications have always been in wide circulation. But these tales of adventure and moral tales of the past have no resemblances with the modern short story.

The history of the modern short story is almost as old as the history of magazines. The recognized body of writing which assumed the name of short story emerged and developed with the rise of periodicals in the nineteenth century. Although story telling in the form of fairy and folk tales dates back to the ancient times, the short story as it exists today, with a conscious form, is not more than a hundred years old.

Short story in the hands of the modern masters is a perfect work of art. As an artistic form, it has undergone a gradual evolution and has developed into a popular form of modern literature. The modern short story writer is an artist, who is a close observer of life, a keen student of character, and a master of style. Every subject, between heaven and earth, is now regarded fit for the short story and it can be told in any manner which may please the artist.

There are at least three distinct stages in the growth of the short story as a modern literary form. All these stages are autonomous and self-sufficient but inter related. The first stage belongs to that of anecdotes and the second that of tales and fables. The third stage emerged in the 19th century with the advent of journals and periodicals which encouraged the growth of character sketches and reportage of incidents. There was yet another stage which belonged to the novella or short fiction. The short story distinct from anecdotes, tales, sketches, reportage and novellas came at the last stage of the evolution of narratives. As a form, it shares some features of these four but it developed its own distinctiveness identified by the presence of a conscious narrative, foregrounding a particular incident, or a situation, or a moment of emotional intensity.

The short story, as a literary genre, has a unique position in the modern era. In the fast moving society in which nobody has enough time to do anything, spending more time on a particular activity is out of agenda for most of the people. Such a social situation has given rise to the popularity of short story as one can satisfy one's literary urge within the limits of time at his or her disposal. Its popularity can be accounted for in many ways, perhaps the chief being the many other demands upon the leisure of the modern reader, which in its turn has assisted the vast development of the magazine containing several complete stories in one issue. Broadcasting, too, has played some part in its success.

As stated earlier, any subject beneath the sky forms the subject matter of a short story. The fractured female identity that struggles to break out of centuries of enforced silence also formed a major subject in many short stories. The "undernourished" woman's silence finds a crystallized form in the short text. The short fiction form, which can best be termed as 'truncated novel', is a tool for the female artist who forges a language, chisels a flexible form and mirrors an experience that reflects the rhythm of the body and the mind. Both for poetic and economic reasons the short story form leads itself to the kaleidoscope of female images that arrange and rearrange themselves in various patterns that are complementary and contradictory to one another.

The historical relativity of human experiences is absorbed into the personal female experiences of the woman writer who writes her story. It is in this context, that the protean and flexible nature of the short story becomes significant. More than any other literary form, the short story has always defied classification and regulations. By the very nature of this lack of rigid structure, the woman writer mentally frees herself from a traditionally bound form and language. She identifies herself with formlessness, accepts a circular and holistic framework that becomes for her a loosely strung chain upon which she beads her fantasy and her experiences. Thus, the woman writer identifies a spatial context and begins to explore and experiment with her hitherto muted experiences. Where the novel in its form embraces a linear structure and a patriarchal tradition, the short story is like a sphere that lifts the woman writer out of linear time and patriarchal logic.

2
WOMEN WRITING

Women's writing was often defined as writing by women, about women and for women. Women's writing now constitutes a powerful articulation of the gender specific concerns of women, whose explicit self-identification as an oppressed group qualifies this branch of writing for analysis as a separate category. Women's writing throws up all kinds of queries related to oppression and colonization. It had helped both to build and express the idea of a female and dismantle the concept of the all-inclusive male. Women's literature, which has evolved out of women's identity struggles, creates a new awareness in men and women.

Literature by women was being written in Britain as far back as the middle ages. Most of this literature was in the form of diaries, autobiographies, letters, protests, stories and poems. However, most women writing before 1800 did not see their writing as an aspect of their female experience or an expression of it. Women's writing has been slow to come into its own for several reasons. There were not enough women writers and they had not enough access to education to make their writing possible; history has ignored and submerged their contributions, their work has been dismissed as concerned with a limited world of experience as they were confined to domestic life.

Women's writing has also been dismissed as hardly of any consequence because religions and political thought had assigned them a place of subordination and labelled them as beings less rational and intellectual than the male of the species. The act of writing enabled them to move outside the narrow role of man's help meet, outside the role of the seductress, the angel or the witch. It helps to problematize the areas of conflict and facilitates a search for alternative models. Women as they deconstruct literary forms and politico-social constructs continue to struggle with the ghosts of their fathers and the inheritance of their mothers. And they invite the reader to do the same.

In India, more than in other country, women writers employ their literary skills and their works of fiction to explore gender related issues and problems. In the Indian context women's fiction is not a pure, creative act of writing, but it is more a mirror of the social conditions. In this specific case, the definition "women's writing" does not appear to be sexist or racist. On the contrary, it focuses the necessary attention on women and their writing.

Fiction today is seriously concerned with changing perception of human relationships, especially man-woman relationship. The family during the last few decades has been under a process of social change, thus substantially affecting the man-woman relationship. This social relationship is marked in the societies of these countries and it has touched the fingers of the family and this interaction has brought a significant change in the structure and various relationships in a family unit. There is a conspicuous change in the spheres of roles and values. From the sociological point of view, the role of husband-wife is the principal component in a family context that has undergone a vital change due to growing enlightenment and the movement for emancipation of women. In this regard, literature has played a sterling role in raising the reader's consciousness. In various forms, it has provided a glimpse into female psyche and dealt with full range of female experience. It portrays, without inhibitions, the new woman who refuses to play a second fiddle to her husband in various walks of life.

Literature is commonly seen as offering its own unique insights into a period. These unique insights come as much from women's pens as from those of men. The last four decades of the present century witnessed a burgeoning of women writers that disprove the hegemonic myth which makes literary creation a male domain and literary discourse a patriarchal privilege. Woman is no longer a mere sign in the writing of men, nor is she merely the muse, the idealized inspiration of the masculine artist and thinker, who may be the all-pervasive aesthetic procreator and the father of the text and whose pen is his instrument of generative power. Instead, woman is a creator herself and an imaginative being whose discourse is a subversion of her silence and whose speech is a challenge to her peripheral status. Among the various perspectives that run through women's texts, that of their gender, transforms their writing into a definite subtext. Their discourse acquires its own identity and recognition. Women's literature is the voice of a group of people who have remained oppressed, ignored and rejected by centuries of biases and vested political interests of the dominant males who, always aligns with each other, reduce womanhood to typical characteristics of inadequacy, impurity, frailty and eternal silence.

The big change in women's writing came with the 1970s when women writers started to transform their own experiences as women as well as their feminity into literary expression. The historical and puranic themes were replaced by the new women. The generation of women writers form the 1970s broke with the past literary tradition. These women writers were more concerned with the individual rather than social or collective issues. In the 1970s with the emergence of the new women, there was shift from the collective to the personal, from the communal to the individual. This shift is clearly expressed by the quest for identity and by the questing female protagonist which characterises the urban middle class writing of the 1970s and the 1980s. Many contemporary women writers describe the conflict between modernity and tradition.

When women wrote, they touched upon experiences rarely touched upon by men, and they spoke in different ways about these experiences. They wrote about childbirth, about house work, about relationships with men, about friendships with other women. They wrote about themselves as girls and as mature women, as wives, mothers, widows, lovers, workers, thinkers and rebels. They also wrote about themselves as writers and about the discrimination against them and the pain and courage with which they faced it.

The short story form best expresses the fractured female identity that struggles to break out of centuries of enforced silence. All that has up surged within the consciousness of the undernourished woman's silence finds a crystallized form in the short text. The truncated novel, ie; short story form, is a tool for the female artist who forges a language, chisels a flexible form and mirrors an experience that reflects the rhythm of the body and the mind. Both for poetic and economic reasons the short story form lends itself to the kaleidoscope of female images that arrange and rearrange themselves in various patterns that are complementary and contradictory to one another.

The historical relativity of human experiences is absorbed into the personal female experiences of the woman writer who writes her story. It is in this context, that the protean and flexible nature of the short story becomes significant. More than any other literary form, the short story has always defied classification and regulations. By the very nature of this lack of rigid structure, the woman writer mentally frees herself from a traditionally bound form and language. She identifies herself with formlessness, accepts a circular and holistic framework that becomes for her a loosely strung chain upon which she beads her fantasy and her experiences. This, the woman writer identifies a spatial context and begins to explore and experiment with her hitherto muted experiences. Where the novel in its form embraces a linear structure and a patriarchal tradition, the short story is like a sphere that lifts the woman writer out of linear time and patriarchal logic.

In the last two decades, more women writers have turned to the short story or rather more appropriately labelled "short text", to express the poetry in their selves. The potentialities latent in the short text have been explored with greater intensity in the past few years.

Contemporary women writers are concerned with the conflicts between art and love, between self-fulfilment and duty. They have insisted upon the right to use vocabularies previously reserved for male writers and to describe formerly taboo areas of female experience. For the first time anger and sexuality are accepted not only as attributes of realistic characters but also as sources of female creative power. Contemporary women writers are aware of their place in a political system and their connections with other women. Like Virginia Woolf and the novelists of the female aesthetic, women writers today, see themselves as trying to unify the fragments of female experiences through artistic vision, and they are concerned with the definition of autonomy for the woman writer.

Changes in the socio-economic conditions have changed our patriarchal attitudes to gender and this contemporary change is reflected in literature too. Baranskaya and Kamala Das in their works, present an image of woman which is totally different form the image of the past, according to which woman was viewed as 'an evil counterfeit, 'a week vassal'

3
WOMEN STORY TELLERS – RUSSIAN SCENARIO

The Russian women had a difficult time to find a voice in literature. The first half of the 18ᵗʰ century saw the publication of occasional imaginative texts by women writers. The reign of Catherine II marked a turning point in women's uplifting. With the improvement in education as well as economic status, women began to get actively involved in writing. According to Belinsky, women's writing in a serious sense began with the Pushkin generation. The female writers came to the fore in the 1830s and 1850s.

The early period (1820-1880) in Russian literature was the age of Romanticism and Realism. In the 1830s, as Russian letters shifted from poetry to prose, women like men began publishing prose in large numbers and by 1850s women's fiction attained new prominence. The period between 1820 and 1840 saw the reign of ''Society tale''- a genre which is indigenous and drew from the emerging Russian literary tradition. It is generally considered that this particular genre have gained women entry to the field of literature as both authors and characters. Elena Gan (1814-1842) and Maria Zhukova (1804-1855) were two most prominent authors of the late 1830s and early 1840s. Major society tales were Zhukova's *Baron Reichman*, Elena Gan's *Ideal* and Karolina Pavlova's *At the Tea Table* (1859). Zukova's *Evening's on the Karpovka* (1838) was a complicated experiment in narration that explores the transition from oral to written storytelling. Nadazhda Durova (1783-1866) most famous for her account of her years in the army during the Napoleonic wars, published prose fiction roughly contemporaneously with Gan and Zhukova. Most of Durova's works evidence a marked Gothic influence and indicate a fascination with the non-Russian. This includes the sympathetic focus on the Tatars in the historical and gender-bending tale *Nurmeka* (1839), the Lithuanian myths in *Gudishk*i (1839), the Polish Gothic in *Pavlion (*1839) and the Jewish-Muslim parents and brothers in *Klad* (1840). Even more than national origin, gender is a remarkably fluid category in many of Durova's works.

The next major period in women's writing was the 1850s, a period of tight censorship, during which authors like the Nadeshda Khvoshchinskaya (1824-1889), Avdotia Panaeva (1819-1893), Sokhanskaya and Marko Vovchok (1833-1907) published some of their best works. These works expand many of the themes and styles of the 1830s. They are treated as 'elaborated society tales'. Writers of the elaborated society tales describe the inner lives of their female protagonists in detail, as also society's artificiality. Evgenia Tur's *A Mistake*, Sokhanskaya's *A Conversation after Dinner*, Panaeva's *Women's Lot* are examples of this genre. The dominance of society tales was soon challenged and over thrown by another type of story set in the provinces rather than in the metropolis-they are the "provincial tales". The provincial tales are concerned with women's lives set in the provinces or countryside. From 1850s many writers belonging to the provincial gentry like Sofia Soboleva, Avdotia Panaeva concentrate on women's personal worlds. The provincial tale was the Russian genre which can be called a literature of women's liberation. The provincial tales clearly articulated women's dissatisfaction with patriarchal society and suggested ways how to escape the problems. Major works belonging to this category are Zhukova's *The Medallion*, Gan's *A Futile Gift*, Panaeva's *The Talni*kov *Family.*

The period from 1881-1917 was the period of transition from Realism to Modernism. Several talented realist writers of the period like Olga Shapir (1850-1916) and Lubove Gurevich were active feminist and the development of new feminist ideologies, more sophisticated and complex than the past made itself felt throughout the realist writing of the period. Olga Shapir's *The Settlement* (1892) is a very good story about peasants who try to better themselves through education, only to find them discriminated against by both the upper classes and their own class. The other works of Olga Shapir were *The Story Years and Avdotya's Daughters* (1898). Bella Ulanovskaya's *Journey to Kashgar* (1973-1989) also represents the best of the Russian long short story. Its chronicler narrator attempts to explain how a woman from Leningrad comes to be executed in Turan, in south eastern Turkestan. The story is rich, both in terms of its realistic detail and its evocative, self-conscious style; it is a fine example of Russian post modernism. Heroines of many works are members of revolutionary, populist groups. Anastasiya Verbitskaya's (1861-1928) *The History of a Life*, is an example. Another important characteristic of the feminist texts of the period was the difference in the attitude to the institution of marriage and marital relationships. Many stories portray the problems of sexual dissatisfaction and heterosexual relationship as a requirement. Maria Krestovskaya's (1862-1910) *The Wail* (1900) and Dmitreva's *The Picnic* (1901) are examples of these types. The year after 1880 saw women realists attaining equal status with their male counterparts. Their texts become empirical and complex.

The year of Socialist Realism (1918-1954) is also known as the era of Stalinism. In 1930 Stalin declared that the "woman question has been solved". The New Soviet woman was a fusion of worker, wife, and mother-a super woman. Ekaterina Strogova's *Women Folk* (1927) is a series of sketches depicting the women workers of a textile factory. Anna Prismanova, best known as a poet of the first wave of immigration to Paris in the 1920s is represented not only by two of her poems but by a brief, rather limited short story, *About the Town and the Vegetable Garden* first published in 1966.

The Bolshevik cultural policy encouraged and trained groups of people of humble origin mainly from provinces, giving them education and professional opportunities and this new arts groups were grateful and loyal to the policies of the state and Stalin. Among them were prose writers like Anna Karavaeva, Lidiya Seifullina (1889-1954) and Vera Inber (1890-1972). The "positive heroine" of the literature of the period is normally woman worker equal to her male counterpart in self-confidence and determination. The "negative characters" are bourgeois women who are unable to adjust to the new social and cultural realities.

From mid-thirties "maternity" becomes an important element in soviet fiction, by women. There is an insistence on the part of the state that women should be productive as well as reproductive. ie; women should contribute to the cause of industrialization and perform duties of a woman. Stories of 40s depict breast feeding mothers and factory workers. Anna Karavaeva's *Rose My Rose* and *Mother Land* depict these themes.

Lidiya Seifullina's works are characterised by a penchant for realism, her stories are short narratives about the violence and confusion of the emerging new order in the village. Her portrait of soviet women, struggling to become independent and free have found their rightful place in the gallery of Russian women characters. Her *Mulch* (1922) was a story of the civil war depicting the violent class struggle in a village. Her *The Lawbreakers* was about the homeless children of the early revolutionary period.

Vera Inber began her literary career shortly before the Bolshevik revolution and is considered one among the classics of Soviet literature. In the 1940s her writing is devoted to the war theme. Her most famous publication of the period is a story almost three years about her life during the Leningrad blockade. Her stories depict the social turmoil during revolution, industrialization and World War II. A noteworthy theme in Inber's writing is that of women's liberation under the Soviet rule.

There were a large number of stories dealing with the psychological dilemmas of ordinary people, domestic life portrayed as a trap and heroines suffered total distress and alienation. There is a shift from "escape plot" to "melancholy tale of failure". Works of Aleksandra Damanskaya, Nadeshda Teffi (1872-1952), Lidia Chukovskaya (1907-1996) are examples.

Nadeshda Teffi described the absurdity of man and expressed the wish to escape to a better world. Teffi's contribution to the traditionally male dominated field of satire is significant. Her earlier stories were reprinted in three collections, *Humorous Stories, Smoke without Fire* and *The Carousel*. Although satire and grotesque predominate in these stories, a note of sadness and lyrical mood are also present.

The death of Stalin in 1953 was followed by another period of relaxed restrictions in Soviet life and literature called the Post Stalin period. With Stalin's death the official method of socialist realism fell into disrepute and other literary methods were sought to replace it. Post Stalinist women's prose works have largely been characterised by a return to themes such as home, family, romance and descriptions of daily life shown of their Stalinist vanishing. The tendency to de-Stalinize romance, many post-Stalinist women writers have sought to reclaim and recoup the lost family. Many of their fictions are, in fact, domestic narratives reflecting the shift of ideological winds away from the nationalist myth of the 'great Stalinist family' back to the 'personal nuclear family'. This is not to say that there was an absence of domestic novels during the Stalin period; where as in the Stalinist period the home and domestic life become mirror reflections of the state, in post Stalinist women's writing the home and family once again occupy centre stage, and the focus shifts to give greater credence to female protagonists inner life and psychological travails.

The post war era (1945) proved to be a propitious moment for all Soviet women writers. This is perhaps the first period in Russian literature when women signify as a major and distinctive group. Three women, Vera Panova (1907-1973), Antonia Koptiaeva (1909-1991) and Galina Nikolaeva (1911-1963), were recipients of the Stalin prize. Vera Panova's wonderfully low-key portraits of children and young people, embedded in her novels and proffered singly in such novellas as *Serezha* (1955), *Valya* (1959), and *Volodya* (1959) underscore the values of good parenting and simple childhood pleasures in lieu of politically correct education. Panova's particular rewriting of the war experience entails domesticating space as well as character. The main setting of *The Train* (1945) already indicates the move from "masculine" battlefield to a site of human repair and recuperation.

In the 1950s a good deal of works by women portrayed heroic past, narrating stories of Second World War. But with the beginning of 1960s women writers began to expand on the path chosen by Panova. Elena Sergeevna's (Grekova) (1907-1996) *Under the Streetlight* (1962) and *The Ladies Hairdresser* (1963) portrayed women of above average standing, whose mistakes lead to psychological perceptions. Grekova is usually regarded by critics as a "Socialist realist with a human face". Her works counter traditional assumptions about woman's place in Soviet society. Grekova is unique in being the first to describe unaffected daily routine of the Soviet Scientific intelligentsia. The other works of

Grekova are *Beyond the Gates* (1962), *No Smiles* (1970), *In Hotel Manage*r (1976) and *The Ship of Windows*.

Nina Katerli (b.1934) was an activist against anti-Semitism. Her early stories were rooted in autobiographical experiences, with time. Her cast of characters covers the full spectrum of old, middle-aged young, and adolescent of both sexes. Her collection of short stories *Windows* (1981) contains most of her stories. Katerli's other works are *The Monster* and *The Barsukov Triangle* (1981).

Glasnost marked a veritable bloom in women's culture, witnessing the debut of several notable literary talents. In the 1970s a new generation of women writers headed by Lyudmila Petrushevskaya (b.1938) come to public attention. Others belonging to this group are Natalia Baranskaya (1908-2004), Ludmila Ulitskaya (b.1943), Nina Gorlanova (b.1947), Nina Sadur (b.1950), Tatiana Tolstaya (b.1951) and Svetlana Vasilenko (b.1956).

Lyudmila Petrushevskaya's works are characterised by an atmosphere of relentless, irreparable despair and her methods are grotesque, that her reader should realise what miserable creatures her characters are. She prevents her narrators from moralising, thus leaving her readers to make their own conclusions. Her first volume of stories *Immortal Love* narrates incidents from the miserable lives of average Muscovites, predominantly women, on the brink of a nervous breakdown. In many of her stories the woman mother is not only lonely, but selfish also. In the stories, *Xenia's Daughter, This Little Girl, A Case of Virgin Birth*, the image of maternity has become a destructive force. Thus she undermines traditional ideas of maternity and dismantles the idea that self-fulfillment of women lies in motherhood.

Natalia Baranskaya came to writing quite late in life, after retiring from her career as a Museum researcher. Her *A Week Like Any Other* (1969) caused great sensation and was immediately hailed as a long overdue examination of the plight of soviet women. Baranskaya's *Remembrance Day* interweaves the fates of seven women during and after the year. Besides these works, Baranskaya had published a collection of stories and novellas under the title *A Negative Gizelle* (1977) and another *Woman with an Umbrella* (1981), followed by *Portrait Presented to a Friend* (1982). Many of her heroines are survivors of the terror and they refuse to act and think in the way that is expected of them. Diversity of character and experience belonging to a wide variety of contexts and ambiguity are the main features of her work.

Ludmila Ulitskaya, one of the most popular writers of post-soviet period is a proponent of "art for art". Her writings are a protest against inclusion of ideology and morality in literature. She took up writing seriously only after glasnost. The major theme of her works is love; she explores love in its diverse manifestations. Her focus is on the female body and female sexuality. Her famous works are *Sonechka (*1995), *Gulia, Lialia's House* and W*omen's Lies* (2003).

Nina Gorlanova is a modern short story writer and novelist. In her works she creates a somewhat fantastic world populated with curious characters and possessing its own mythology. Her main themes are maternity, hardships of everyday chores of typical Russian women, life of provincial intelligentsia. Her short novel *Love in Rubber Gloves* won first prize in the International Cope of women's prose.

Nina Sadur's works are marked by excessive violence and folkloric fantastic themes. *She Who Bears No Grudge* (1990) and *Witch's Tears* (1994) are her two short story collections.

Descended from a highly literary family, Tatiana Tostayais the great grand niece of Lev Tolstoi and the great grand- daughter of Aleksei Tolstoi. Her story *Peters* established her reputation as a unique, original, stylist among writers of the young generation. Language, imagination and time are the most important elements of Tolstaya's fiction. Her characters seek escape from their disappointments in dreams, which provide them a temporary shelter, escape for a few m*oments*. Her major works include *Sweet Shura* (1983), *Fakir* (1986), *Night* (1987), *On the GoldenPorch* (1988) and *Sleep Walker in a Fog* (1992).

Svetlana Vasilenko belongs to the generation of Russian writers who began their literary careers in the interregnum between the late stagnation-the end of Leonid Ilich Brezhnev's rule and perestroika. Her outspoken and self-conscious female characters, the personal tone of her narration, and her masterful use of metaphorical language instantly made her a name among critics and colleagues. One of her best works is *Shamara and other Stories.*

Since most Russian women writers are not interested in advancing the cause of militant feminism as it is understood in the west, 'women's prose' is characterised by an intuitive approach to human problems. In practical terms that means that in the works of women writers the narrators and protagonists are usually women. The prose of most contemporary women authors can be recognised by its sensitivity, emotional tone, and personal touch. Moreover issues of love and marriage, family and infidelity, children and parenthood are always at the centre of narratives by women authors. It does not mean, of course, that the prose of female writers is thematically limited.

The prose of the contemporary Russian women writers is little different from that of their male counterparts. The better known Russian women writers are today rarely involved in issues which concern representatives of western ideological feminism. Instead they concentrate on the investigation of the female character, and on the problems that Russian women face in their daily lives. Single motherhood, sexuality, infidelity, and loneliness, as well as the economic conditions of Russian women in the post-soviet era are the core of their works.

4
WOMEN STORY TELLERS – MALAYALAM SCENARIO

It was with the nationalist movement that a powerful female emerged in Indian literature. In the years after independence, there has been visible progress in the literacy of women, even though they rank lower everywhere. Women in Kerala have a much better position where literacy is concerned, in comparison with their counterparts in other states in India. The topic of women's writing is poorly addressed in traditional literary histories. The first half of the twentieth century saw two women writers Lalithambika Antharjanam (1909-1987) and K. Saraswathy Amma (1919-1965) figuring prominently in the field of short story writing. But it is quite possible that they might have been preceded by others who actively engaged the space allotted to them by the women's magazines, a number of which began to appear in Kerala since the late nineteenth century. Much of what the women wrote then belongs to the traditional genres of 'Keerthana's', 'Kaikotikali songs', 'Sthothra's' etc.

Among the woman writers in Malayalam, Lalithambika Antharjanam is chronologically the first and undoubtedly one of the best. She was extraordinarily gifted with the ability to narrate stories with intensity of feeling and in poetic language. Antharjanam's short stories reflect a duality: the duality of a woman caught between two types of emotions-the individualistic and the socialistic. The individualistic concerns arise from the caring, nurturing, creative and harmonious instincts of love, compassion and humaneness. The socialistic expressions are aroused by the indignant, reformist, revolutionary ideas couched in protest by the oppressed, exploited community of women. These conflicting emotions prevent her from being aggressively feminist. She evolves a form of women's writing which is totally opposed to the injustices perpetrated against women, but hesitates to give up love and tenderness, innate feminine qualities, while fighting for her rights.

In *Moodupadathil*, the first in the collection of that title (1946), she tells the story of a self-sacrificing Namboodiri woman being suffocated within the four walls of her house. Most of the seven stories included in *Thakarna Thalamura* (1949) are concerned with the miseries befalling Namboodiri women as a result of the tradition-ridden marriage system prevailing in the community. Her stories have opened the eyes of the thinking section of people belonging to all communities and earned her their unstinted encomium. Some of her other well-known collections, numbering over a dozen, are *Adyathe Kathakal* (1937), and *Gramabalika* (1968).

The stories of Lalithambika Antharjanam are remarkable in the sense that they initiated a process, not of explicitly challenging but subtly interrogating the glorified ideals of womanhood, domesticity, motherhood and marital fidelity. The questions of the interrelations of religion, social norms and gender were ingeniously incorporated into the text of her stories to offer an alternative identity for women. Her characters stepped out of the constricted space traditionally allotted to women but never radically disrupted the societal ideals.

The stories of K. Saraswathi Amma (1919-1975) mirror the special joys and, even more, the sorrows of women. They have generally added to the aesthetic pleasures of readers for her language is only a medium to convey her ideas. Her story *Sthrijanmam* smacks of women's bitterness and indignation against male domination. Through the medium of the short story she constantly strives to uproot patriarchal values and expose their one-sidedness and hypocrisy. What is amazing in her stories is her avowed denunciation of patriarchy and the uncompromising stances that her protagonists reveal. Her characters are protagonist of her ideology. Her other collections include *Penbuddhi, Vivahasammanam* and *Cholamarangal.* She did not take her life, but she lived single and isolated. Her work applauded only after her death.

Another writer Sarala Rama Varma in her collections *Navamukulam* and *Kathakadamban* deal with love between man and woman. While vividly delineating love marriages and domestic life with its entire vicissitudes, she also seems to suggest methods of reforming the marital system.

The stories of Rajalakshmi (1930-1965) question the ambiguous representation of womanhood as a sacrificial entity for familial relationships. She wrote about father- daughter relationships and the choking effects of patriarchal effects have upon women, particularly those who were accomplished and imaginative. The serial publication of her novel Uchaveyilum Illam Nilavum was cancelled because of protest from readers who found her attack on the hypocrisy of idealist men too close to home. She found it impossible to continue her writing career and took her life. Death is a haunting theme in her works. Some of her stories are *Aathmahathya, Maappu, Parajitha* and *Oru Adyapika.*

Born in the Nalappad family rich with literary and cultural traditions Madhavikutty (1934-2009) known also as Kamala Das after her marriage, was very different from other women short story writers in her style and content and her approach to writing is very individualistic, and modern and in some ways not indigenous to Kerala. Her characters are unusual people who follow their inner instincts and try to unravel their identity. Kamala Das brings a new language and spirit to the modern Malayalam short story. Though at first it may seem to have imbibed a great deal of the external influence of English and Western literature, by its sheer individuality and truthfulness to the modern Indian scenario, it integrates the western influence with Indian moorings. In a very complex way it retains its identity as Indian and even Keralites. She, through her stories shocked the society into a traumatized acknowledgement of the sexuality and physical needs of women. *Neypayasam* (1962), *Koladu* (1969), *Chekkerunna Pakshikal* (1999), *Ente Pathakal* (1999) are some of her famous works.

P. Vatsala (b.1938) is a noted contemporary novelist and short story writer in Malayalam literature. Her works reveal a happy departure from tradition and are marked by a fresh social outlook. Many of her stories are potent discussions of the double oppression endured by the repressive patriarchal values of gender as well as by those of a coercive subalternity of caste. *Kayam, Neelamma, Thulabharam, Pookkuveyil, Ponveyil, Madakkam* etc. are some of her stories.

Sara Joseph (b.1949), well known feminist writer in Malayalam, is a prolific writer who has established herself as a short story writer and a novelist. She has retold many puranic stories from a feminist perspective, with the aim of liberating minds conditioned belief in stereotypes and distortions of women. Many of her stories problematize gender identity by juxtaposing the socially constructed selves of women with their real selves. Some of her stories are *Manassile Thee Mathram* (1973), *Kadinte Sangeetham* (1975), *Paapathara, Nilavu Ariyunnu, Puthuramayanam.*

The nineteen eighties ushered in a host of notable women short story writers like Ashitha, Chandramati, Gracy, B. M. Suhara, Githa Harinarayan, Priya A. S., C. S. Chandrika, K. R. Mallika, K. P. Sudheera, Sitara, K. R. Meera etc.

Ashitha is a notable short story writer known for sensitive portrayal of life. She uses meaningful silences to condense the story and preserve its integrity of theme. *Apoorna Viramangal* is one of her notable stories. Chandramati the pen name of B. Chandrika is an intellectual with doctorate in English literature. Her stories are an unusual blend of thought and emotion. Her story *Kavithayude Katha* suits the contexts as it serves to unveil the hardships of a housewife trying to cope with an unexpected burst of creativity.

Gracy is a major woman writer who believes that writing is a natural and non-genderistic activity. Her stories are force arguments for the elimination of oppressive traditional restrictions on women and the expansion of the woman's space in the private as well as the public spheres. In her one-page story about the *Parable of the Sower,* Gracy brings in a broad narrative of context of contemporary drug culture and the pseudo-religious cults of Westernized gurus. Her first collection of short stories *Padiyirangiya Parvathi,* was published in 1991. Her *Paanchali* won the best Katha prize for the best Malayalam short story of 1998.

The notable stories of B. M. Suhara are *Kinavu* (1990), *Mozhi* (1991), *Iruttu* (1994). Githa Harinarayan who passed away at an early age has left behind two collections of short stories that portray her individual style. All her stories are infused with a love of life and sense of fun that is unique. The story *Asanghaditha*, which means a woman not included in any union; has all the special characteristics of Gita's writings. Priya A. S. is a young writer whose stories reflect the dreams and aspirations of the younger generation. The story *Swapnanoolukal* by its very title testifies this. She weaves a colourful tapestry of fantasy and reality to depict a woman's feeling of alienation.

C. S. Chandrika had already established herself as a strong feminist before she turned to the short story as a medium of communication. Though a few in number, her stories have the distinct flavour and force of her personal beliefs. The story *Nilavum Sarpangalum*, is a complicated narrative of women's sexual desires, inseparably linked with her feeling of love. K. R. Mallik's works include *Amma, Valayam* and *Nirangalkkappuram*. K. P. Sudheera's collections of short stories are *Neelakkadambu* and *AaroOral*. Sitara is the latest entrant into the literary field and has been successful in replacing the timid, tradition bound woman of yesterday with the bold, vivacious, independent girl of today. The story *Agni* portrays a girl of today, facing one of the pertinent problems of the times. K. R. Meera (b.1970) won Kendra Sahithya Akademy Award in 2009 for her short story *Ave Maria. Ormayude Njarambu, Moha Manja, Malakhayude Marukukal and Soorpanakha* are some of her other stories.

The contemporary literature portrays without any hesitation the new woman, who refuses to be a toy in the hands of men. The 'glorified' woman is now replaced by 'real' woman with wishes, wants and desires. The women writers have introduced realism in their stories. The conceptual issues involved are purity and virtue in relation to sex and marriage, the assertion of the 'self' as against abnegation of the self and self-indulgence as against self-denial. Literature, by reflecting the 'new woman' contributes to consciousness rising and helps women to overcome the sense of isolation which has been one of the main instruments of their oppression in patriarchal society. The liberated woman is aware of the choices open to her. This awareness frees her form the compulsiveness of traditional role-playing and at the same time awakens her to the complexity of living and loving. To be fully human is to face the hardness of her life with strength and hope, to substitute fearful compliance with conscious and to shatter the internal victimization by learning self-acceptance.

5
NATALYA BARANSKAYA AS THE MIRROR OF EARLY RUSSIAN FEMINISM

Natalya Vladimirovna Baranskaya, a Soviet writer of short stories, was born on 31ˢᵗ December 1908 at St. Petersburg in Russia. She was born into a family whose concern was revolutionary activity. Her parents were engaged in underground work. She along with her parents migrated first to Switzerland and then to Germany for political reasons. In 1914 she returned to Russia with her mother. Her father, who had never married her mother, remained in Germany.

In 1929 Baranskaya graduated from Moscow State University with degrees in Philology and Ethnology. Her professional life after graduation includes work in the publishing field and in various museums. Her husband was an Army Captain and was killed in the Battle of Kursh in August 1943. After that she raised their two daughters alone and also attended part-time post-graduate school and earned yet another degree. She never remarried. The final eight years of her working life was spent in Pushkin Museum, where she developed an intense interest in the poet Pushkin and more significantly, in his wife Natalia Goncharova. Baranskaya retired from Pushkin Museum in 1966.

After Baranskaya's retirement at the age of 56 she began writing. Her fascination to the great poet Pushkin and his wife has resulted in her two works - *The Colour of Dark Honey* (1977) and *A Portrait*

Presented to a Friend (1982). In 1969 she published her masterpiece *A Week Like any Other.* This story is translated into several languages. This story caused great sensation and was immediately hailed as a long overdue examination of the plight of Soviet Women. Baranskaya herself mentions that "there had been nothing written, either as fiction or fact, about how hard life was for our women, who legally have equal rights with men". The story does not in any way oppose the Soviet System; it simply states that this is the way women live, which is not healthy for them, their families or their society.

Baranskaya's most substantial text *Remembrance Day* interweaves the fates of seven women during and after the war. It is one of the few fictional texts by Russian women writers to place the hardships of the war, the traumatized condition which the women have endured during the war. These women's life histories add up to a reasonably full account of ordinary women's experience in the Stalin years. Although the subject is war, typically a male-dominated activity, it serves more as a vehicle for examining the life experiences of the main characters, all of whom are women. The narrative traces the psychological and physical journeys of seven women to the graves of their men, who perished during the war. In the course of the novel, an eighth woman silently accompanies them, the "Woman in black", she is invisible to everyone expect the women and she is present throughout, she is Baranskaya herself.

Baranskaya concerns herself exclusively with female characters and their plight, but her concerns transcend gender boundary. She is occupied with the larger question of war, the nature of humanity and its future. For Baranskaya, the war and society are impersonal structures whose effects can only be true, if felt personally. The suffering and grief endured by her characters are personal but they are reduplicated endlessly and hence attain universal dimensions.

Besides these works, Baranskaya has published a collection of stories and novellas under the title *"A Negative Gizelle"* in 1977, *"Women with an Umbrella"* in 1981 followed by *"Portrait Presented to a Friend"* in 1982, *Lubka, the Kiss, The Petunin Affair* etc. *The Petunin Affair,* told from a man's point of view, reveals the petty side of Soviet bureaucrats, while *Lubka* traces the reformation of a juvenile delinquent. Her most recent work *"Autobiography without Omissions"* appeared in 1990.

Baranskaya's experiences are reflected in her interest in working women with children – it is a recurring theme in these stories, which were published from 1969 to 1986. Baranskaya's focus jumps from character to character, and her stories develop slowly, through action and detail. The narrow-minded hypocrisy of those who dictate how others should behave is a recurrent theme in many of her stories. Baranskaya's representation of women is more multi-faceted. Rather than standing aside from power struggles of men, many of Baranskaya's women get involved in these power struggles, sometimes, as victims, sometimes as executioners. In narrative structure Baranskaya follows the devices of traditional realism, ambiguous closed ending, a resolution and emphasis on unexpected twists in human behaviour.

It has to be admitted that Baranskaya's work led to a certain revival of interest in women's issues in literature and one can find its reflections in the work of Petrushevskaya, Tolstaya and many others.

Baranskaya passed away in October 2004.

6
KAMALA DAS AS INDIAN FEMINIST WRITER

Kamala Das has been hailed as the new woman of Indian writing in English. She was a poet, novelist, short story writer and essayist. She wrote under various names as Kamala Das, Madhavikutty, and Kamala Suraiya. Her relatives lovingly called her 'Amy'. Each name represented a body of her works, a phase of her life or an aspect of her personality.

Kamala Das was born into an aristocratic Nair Hindu family at Punnayurkulam in Thrissur district, Kerala on March 31, 1934. She was the daughter of V. M. Nair, former managing editor of Mathrubhumi Daily, and poet Nalappat Balamani Amma. Under the influence of her great uncle and writer, Nalappat Narayana Menon, and her mother, and her great grandmother's younger sister called Ammalu, a poetess devoted to Lord Krishna, she started writing poetry at a tender age. Needless to say that hailing from such a family of professional writers, she inherited the skill.

Nalappat, like all matriarchal families was a sisterhood of women. Until recently among the Nair community of Kerala, the matriarchal system was prevalent The Nalappat family to which Kamala was born is such a one. She was born when matriarchy was in its decadent state. In the Nalappat family the only male member was Kamala Das' grand uncle Nalappat Narayana Menon. The name itself suggests that matriliny was followed in the family. 'Nalappat' is the name of his mother 'tharavad' and not that of his father. This was a significant feature of maternal in which the women took their mothers name and even matrilineal uncles as surname. According to this system the women were known as belonging to a particular 'tharavad' and not as the daughter of or wife of a particular man. This gives them an identity of their own unlike in the case of patriliny where a woman is known only in relation to a man. But during Kamala Das' youth there aroused a change in this system. Hence, Kamala Das lived in a matriarchal family having patriarchal ideology. Kamala Das' name itself has a patrilineal touch. The shift towards patrilineal culture was brought in by the demands of the time.

Kamala Das first attended a European school at Calcutta, then the Elementary school at Punnayurkulam and then a boarding school run by the Roman Catholic nuns, but in each of them she stayed for a short while. At the Catholic boarding school, she got ill and was removed to Calcutta where private tutors were engaged to teach her fine arts.

Kamala's parental home was influenced by the movement of Mahathma Gandhi, and its members used to wear Khadi clothes and even spin Khadi yarn, especially her grandmother, to whom this girl was deeply attached in her early age and whom she remembered so sweetly in her later life. Mahathma's photos hung in every room. Even the servants felt his presence in the house and began wearing Khadi. The Nalapatt house, that is how her ancestral home was called, consisted of seven occupants in all, who were her grandmother, her aunt Ammini, her grand uncle, the poet, her great grandmother, her two sisters, and Mahathmaji.

In 1949, at the age of fifteen, Kamala was married to Madhav Das, an official in the Reserve Bank of India, who later went to the United Nations Organisations. He was much elder to her. She was taken to Bombay where her husband lived. As he was experienced in sex with his maid servants, his contact with her was usually cruel and brutal. Her husband had no soothing words for her, no time to spare for her and was ever busy sorting out his files and affixing his signature on them. And as a traditional wife, she was expected to discharge her domestic duties well and to look to the needs and comforts of her husband. This eroded her own distinct personality and dwarfed her forever. She was just sixteen years old when the first of her three sons was born; at eighteen she was a mother and disgruntled wife who began to write obsessively.

Although she and her husband were romantically incompatible, he supported her writing.

Kamala Das whimsically straddled a socio-cultural landscape, exploring daring new beliefs, chasing ephemeral images of youngness and happiness, and continuously shocking people. Myriad aspects of her self coalesce into a winsome whole in her work, the like of which has no parallel in Indian literature. She is the only women poet of Indian writing in English who has attained worldwide recognition. Some of her poems are *Summer in Calcutta* (1965), *The Descnedants* (1967), *My Grandmother's House, The Old Playhouse and Other Poems* (1973). Her works reflects her restlessness as a sensitive woman moving in the male-dominated society and in them she appears as a champion of woman's cause. It is important to note that in her poems she gives a mythical framework to her search for genuine love and identifies it with the Radha-Krishna myth or with the Mira-Krishna relationship.

Kamala Das, who received no formal education, no pompous university degree, is a conscientious artist who is mainly guided by her impulse and instinct for precise and harmonious words. She is fully aware of the value of words and their finer shades of meaning. Kamala Das's prose works form a record of the social set of Kerala, of her childhood days. The physical environment in which Kamala lived is very much a part of all that she has written. The kinship system of the Nair community of those days as presented by her was a very significant one in the society. Its significance lies in the fact that the distinction between 'maternal' and 'paternal' was differentiated in the kinship vocabulary and it had much to do with the family set up.

Varshangalkkumunbu, Balyakalasmaranakal, Diarykkurippukal (1992) and *Neermathalam Poothakalam (1994)* are the major works of Kamala Das set against her ancestral home and covering roughly the third and fourth decades of the 20th century. Even a casual reading of these autobiographical works reveals the unique caste system that prevailed in Kerala which stratified people into various levels depending on the nature of their profession handed down to them from generation to generation. Kamala Das' above mentioned works presents the joint family system of those days. She chose colours from a varied palette, drawing on nostalgic memories of growing up in a central Kerala 'tharavad' surrounded by uncles, aunts, cousins and a bevy of housemaids its air heady with the scent of ripe mangos, guavas, and pomegranates.

Kamala Das's autobiography *My Story* (1976) is the beginning of her exploration and movement into women's experiences. *My Story* is the story of a liberalised woman who has discarded the burdensome travails of tradition and taboos, who has had an eventless childhood and a diseased youth, and who has now matured and turned religious and spiritual in the last leg of her life (The language taboo is associated with words and expressions which are not openly said, for there are restrictions about them, and expressions, which most other writers especially the women writers do not dare to).

Though internationally renowned for the spirited poems in English, Kamala Das has written brilliant short stories in her mother-tongue. Critic and academic M. N. Karassery remarked, "Kamala Das stands out on account of her resourcefulness imagination and uncanny ability to tell the tale". A thematic and structural survey of her prose convinces the reader that she writes it with the same urgency and the same feminine sensibility as she does her verses. Kamala Das had given a new dimension to the Malayalam short stories. Her stories have been known for the realistic portrayal of women's life. She was an iconoclast of her generation who spoke unabashedly about the Indian women's sexual desires. She exposed the hypocrisies of a society living in an illusory world of pseudo morality and oblivious of the stark realities around. Honesty of expression and emotional depth made her the best writer of the Malayalam.

Kamala Das infused the lightness of innocence, force of feminine charm, complexities of the heart and the ineffable allure of simplicity into Malayalam literature through a series of delicately nuanced and daintily sensitive stories. Some of her famous collections of short stories are *Pakshiyude Manam (1964), Naricheerukal Parakkumbol (1966), Thanuppu (1968), Neypayasam (1991), Chekkerunna Pakshikal (1996), Nashtapetta Neelambari (1998), Palayanam (1990), Chandanamarangal (2005), Rukminikkoru Pavakutty* etc.

Though Kamala Das's prose writings are controversial, her essays like, *I Studied All Men, What Women Expect out of Marriage and What They Get, Why Not More Than One Husband, And I*

Have Lived Beautifully tend to consolidate her image in public as feminine. Besides these Kamala has written extensively for various popular magazines and periodicals, such as Opinion, The Illustrated Weekly of India, Poetry East and West, Femina, etc. On December 16, 1999 at the age of 65, she converted to Islam and became Kamala Suraiya.

Kamala Das, who ruled the literary world like a champion of liberty and emancipation, now bids adieu to the physical world at the age of 75. She breathed her last on 31st May, 2009 at a hospital in Pune where she was admitted following respiratory problems. On her last visit to her native place before handing over her own land to Sahithya Academy she mused, "If I have another birth I want to be a bird. I will then fly over this land, sing meticulously and soar to heights". Her supreme soul might have left the physical body but she will live in the hearts of scholarly people and rule the literary world.

7

NATALYA BARANSKAYA – THE CHRONICLER OF WOMEN'S EVERYDAY LIFE

Recent Russian women's fiction points a bleak picture of Russian society, exposes the disintegration of family ties, and communicates vividly the debasing indignities with which Russian women confront daily. Perhaps the single strongest impression conveyed by this fiction is that of an overall lack; of an imprecisely grasped loss or simply an absence of stable, secure identity; of experiences to be surmounted rather than recaptured. In Russia most of the women writers are not interested in advancing the cause of militant feminism as it is understood in the west, women's prose is characterised by an initiative approach to human problems. In the works of women writers the narrators and protagonists are usually women. Natalya Baranskaya's writings can be recognised by its sensitivity, emotional tone, and personal touch. Moreover issues of love and marriage, family and parenthood are always at the centre of narratives by her. The stories of Natalya Baranskaya portray the everyday life of women. Her stories like *The Kiss, Lubka, At Her Father's And At Her Mother's Place, A Week Like Any Other* are simple depiction of women's struggle for survival in the family and society.

The Kiss

Natalya Baranskaya's story *The Kiss* is a story of a widowed mother and daughter. The story portrays a widowed mother who tasted the bitterness of loneliness after the marriage of her one and only daughter.

Nadezhda Mikhailovna, was a senior scholar at the Institute of the USSR Academy of Sciences. No one ever took her for over thirty-five. She was an attractive woman, elegant and lively. Years before in a war she had been separated from her first love. Through the joys and sorrows of family life, with its discord and divorce, followed by single mother hood and work life became a burden to her. She had been dropped, abandoned, castoff or should been dumped. Hence at a very early stage in life itself she became a widow. She didn't get the love and care of a husband. After her only daughter's marriage she lived alone in her one room apartment. Her daughter Natasha ignored her mother's feeling and wishes to get close to the daughter.

So as a woman and as a mother Nadezhda failed to get the love and care which she wished to get. Out of this loneliness she got acquainted to Viktor, a young man. When he kissed her, she could not forbid him because after her husband's death she was untouched by men. So after many years, when touched by a man her womanly feelings awakened. The thought that she was noticed by a young guy made her happy, and there was something a little shameless about her happiness. While they were in the taxi Viktor asked where he should take her, and as soon as the taxi moved off he put his arm around her shoulders, trying to draw her closer to him. She refused to yield, but her heart stopped, then instantly began to pound as it had in the elevator when they involved in a long kiss. But he firmly took her by the arm and moved his knees closer to her legs. She freed herself from his grasp and opened her purse as if to get her handkerchief or wallet. From her behaviour it is clear that Nadezhda was not a woman who was waiting for a chance to flirt with men. She was always conscious about her position. If she was interested in bodily delights, in that taxi itself she might have yielded to him. But Nadezhda was sceptical about men's chivalrous impulses. But her mind was happy in the thought that she was liked by a young guy. That day when she reached her room in the evening, instead of hurrying to bed, she sat down in front of the mirror and began studying her face. She noticed that her slight flush had faded, and her wrinkles had become more pronounced. She took off her beads and her rings, threw off her dress, and went into the bathroom.

As soon as she lay down to sleep, she felt the dry firm lips that had been pressed to her mouth. The memories of their long unthinkable kiss were still there at her lips because the touch by a man for at least twenty years after her husband's death changed her totally. When Viktor informed about his visit to her apartment we can see Nadezhda's preparations to receive him. That day, Nadezhda cleaned the apartment, took a bath, applied a yeast facial mask, and went to bed earlier than usual. Even before she had time to think about what she was going to wear in the evening, she had fallen asleep.

The next day she decided to leave work an hour early in order to prepare for the evening. She still had to do some shopping for supper. She already had her coat on when the phone rang. Her daughter Natasha wanted her to come and visit and spend the night with her because her husband Seriozha would be late. She also told her to buy some fruits for her little daughter.

Nadezhda Mikhailovna disliked disappointing her daughter, but she firmly declared that she couldn't make it. While doing the evenings shopping, she bought some apples and grapes for Natasha as well. At home she put away the fruit and appetizers in the refrigerator, placed the wine out on the balcony, and lay down on her bed for ten minutes, her eyes closed. Then she dressed and went to the kitchen to get everything ready for supper. She sliced the bread, opened some cans, and covered the table with a bright striped table cloth. On it she set some yellow ceramic plates and dark blue cups. She admired the table which looked like spring.

Nadezhda herself thought the fact that she knew nothing absolutely about her guest: his tastes, habits and views. May be on that day she will feel good with him, but didn't know about the next day. She feared he would disappear after spending the night with her and never come back to her. She didn't even know his last name and also not know whether he was married or not. Any way she was sure that she would lose her independence, the carefree ease that usually see in people who work well and relax well.

Even though all these considerations came to her mind it didn't prevent her from carefully and deliberately getting ready to receive her guest. She took her apron off, rubbed some lotion into her hands, and went over to the large mirror to fix her hair and put on her rings and earrings. But a few minutes before the appointed time we can see Nadezhda going to her daughter carrying all the food items and the fruits.

So here we can see that leaving all her desires Nadezhda Mikhailovna was going to her daughter. Till the very last moment we can see Nadezda preparing to receive her guest, but she can't disappoint her daughter. The love and responsibility of a mother towards her daughter changed her mind and she decided to leave all her happiness for Natasha and her little daughter.

Lubka

Lubka is a story of a prodigal daughter and her mother. Lubka was the daughter of a soldier's widow, named Praskovya Egorovna. She left the school at fourteen and she was working in the light bulb factory. Both of them were living in a flat. Lubka had lot of friends and in the flat they all gathered and made disturbances in her room which annoyed the other residents of the flat. In the flat people told awful stories about Lubka; she drank, got mixed up with young boys, didn't study and didn't work. Those who were living under her room could hear her gramophone thundering out. The tramp of the dancers made the chandelier sway and bits of ceiling falling down. Sometimes shouts and crashes could be heard and the neighbours had run to them several times and told them they will call the police.

The neighbours all gathered together to an open sitting of the club's comrade court regarding an appraisal of Lubka Sapozhnikova's behaviour in the light of her disregard of internal house rules and her immoral behaviour. The first two rows were filled with activists in the housing department and people invited by the chairman and also by Lubka's neighbours, who were the plaintiffs. The plaintiff neighbours sat uneasily, waiting for Lubka coming. Mikhail Konnikov had been sent there by the light bulb factory where Lubka worked. The Komsomol organisation had given Mikhail wide ranging powers; if Sapozhnikova was being accused of something serious he was not to fight for her; but if it turned out to be nothing too depraved, and then he could plead for her. At first Mikhail was very attentive, but then, as he was looking at Lubka, his heart suddenly jumped. So he tried not to look at Lubka and concentrated on the toes of his boots.

Zalomin was the court chairperson. Lubka's friends also assembled there. Lubka was already late and that itself was a black mark against her. Lubka swept on to the stage. Her mother came behind her. Lubka moved her chair forward and sat down, almost completely shielding her mother with her body. She took a blue scarf with red poppies from her head, took out of a small mirror and calmly began to adjust her hair. All knew why Lubka had been late. She had been making herself beautiful. She'd got herself up as if for a party. Lubka didn't notice the crowd. She liked sitting there on the stage, as if she were in a play. Even sitting down she was posing, lifting her head, moving her feet in their fashionable high boots with gold decoration.

These all show that she was not at all conscious about what others might think of her. Though she was the accused, she had no change. The victim's statement was very detailed and listed all the excesses committed by Lubka and her guests in the flat after drinking. It talked of the incessant disturbances in the Sapozhnikov's room which annoyed the other residents of the flat. When Zalomin read the statement Lubka didn't listen to it. She already knew from her preliminary talk with the chairman what she was being accused off. She had admitted that everything written about the noisy gatherings and drinking was true. But nothing about the fellows that were meant to have spent the night there was true. She felt secure in the knowledge that they couldn't prove it.

Thus it is clear that Lubka was bold enough to admit the things she had done and to reject what she hadn't. Zalomin wanted Lubka's life style to be changed. It was his duty to stop her ruining her life. Zalomin wanted the co-tenants and all those who knew Lubka and her mother to speak about her. And let her listen to what they were saying. Furthermore, if anybody had anything positive to say, perhaps it would touch some nerve in her; shame her, appeal to her conscience or her pride. When Zalomin announced that Comrade Mikhail Konnikov from the light bulb factory where Lubka works will speak, Mikhail got up. He didn't really want to speak. The more he heard, the statement, the things said by the co-tenants, the more he was convinced that there was no point in trying to defend her. But something prevented him criticising her. He addressed the judges over Lubka's head, without looking at her and said that from the factory's point of view they had no criticism of Lubka Sapozhnikova. She carries out her appointed work satisfactorily. Confused by his lies Konnikov also added that she had only been working for the factory for three months, a rather short period. The last bit was not true. Even Lubka looked at him in amazement. She never got up early in the morning and so she was always late to the factory.

From Mikhail's opinion about Lubka it is clear that Mikhail likes Lubka. That's why he talked in favour of her even though he knew that she was very naughty.

When the judge asked Lubka why she left her school when she was only fourteen years old she remembered how she had come to leave school. It was true that she'd found school difficult, especially in the third form. She couldn't seem to grasp mathematics, physics and chemistry. The mathematics teacher and the physics teacher weren't too bad. But the chemistry teacher was the real pain. She persecuted Lubka because she hated her and she never ever helped her. She would ask her to answer questions more often than the others and set her very difficult problems on purpose.

During a free period they were told not to make any noise or disturbance and not to leave the school. Some read, some did their homework, some played at noughts and crosses. Many just wandered round the school. Lubka left the classroom. She went in search of her classmate Kolya. She was in love for the first time in her life, with Kolya. It was a secret, nobody knew about it, not even him. He was sitting on the stair case which was unused holding a book and pencil. Lubka's heart raced. She went up to him and stopped. He got irritated and asked her what she wants. Hearing this she didn't behave rudely to him as she did to others, instead she softly told him to show her what he was reading. He closed the magazine and showed her the cover, Science and Life. Both of them were looking the pictures in the book. They looked at the pictures for a long time until Kolya's ears and Lubka's cheeks were beginning to burn.

Then the Chemistry teacher on school duty came there and asked them why they were hiding there. Hearing this both of them descended the stairs and stood dejected before the teacher like accused prisoners. They told her that they were looking the pictures in the magazine. All this would have been bearable if she'd left it there, but for some reason she took them to the classroom, opened the door and said, to them that was the place where they should look at pictures and not in dark corners!

There were several children in the classroom and they laughed and gossiped about it. Somebody had drawn a cartoon on the blackboard of Lubka and Kolya kissing, hiding behind a chemistry text book. Kolya began to avoid Lubka, turning away from her when their paths crossed and averting his gaze. Lubka was hurt and annoyed. It wasn't her fault. She developed a perfect hatred of the chemistry teacher and of chemistry, along with physics and mathematics.

From this incident we can understand that there was no fault with Lubka and Kolya. They were simply watching the pictures in the book. A teacher should be a person who leads the students in the right way. But here, instead of trying to understand the students mind, she simply accused them in front of other students. This hurts their young mind very much and Lubka developed a perfect hatred of the chemistry teacher.

Another boy named Senka from 3-A who was re-doing a year had a liking for Lubka. He was really repulsive. At first he just looked at her, and then he began to spout rubbish about her being the prettiest girl in the school. Lubka stopped avoiding him and began listening to what he said with pleasure.

Senka persuaded her to go to a party. There were five boys and four girls from the third year. The fifth was Lubka, Senka's partner. The girls bought fruit juice, but the boys had wine. They drank, danced and played forfeits, with bottles of wine as prizes. Senka always chose her. And then they found themselves a small room where they'd left their coats. The room was dark, cramped and stuffy. Senka pressed Lubka's lips to his and squeezed her so hard that she couldn't move. At first she tried to push him away, to get away herself, but then she relaxed, moaned softly and weakened.

So Senka became her 'first'. He would make excuses to come and see her, saying that he'd help her with mathematics, waiting for the chance. She never loved him. On the contrary, he always repulsed her. After some days Lubka decided to make an end to the relationship with Senka. She would never give way to him again, she wouldn't see him anymore. She didn't go to school, but he came to see her after school. She sent him away by saying that she hates him and not to come to see her anymore. But he did come. She shouted at him snatched a plastic bread board from the table and flung it at his face. She broke his nose. She wanted to kill him. He knocked, and ran off.

Soon whispers started in school. The whisperings encircled Lubka like flies. They were born and multiplied. They buzzed in her ears, rustled behind her back and under her feet like dry leaves. Then one day as Lubka was leaving school with her friends, some older boys, Senka's mates, showered her with streams of foul abuse and obscene jokes. Lubka choked with anger, went up to the boys and lifted her satchel to hit them. She didn't know which one of the three she was aiming at; she wanted to knock out all the three. Two of them got hold of her hands while the third seized her satchel and shuffled round the room with it, hunched up and repeated in a squeaky voice not to hang around with boys.

The boys went on jeering at Lubka till they heard a voice to stop it. It was the P. E. teacher, moving menacingly towards the boys. They chucked Lubka's satchel onto the stage and ran off. She stood there, dishevelled, pathetic. The teacher approached her and said something. His lips moved, he spoke, but she didn't hear a word. Then she started to run. Somebody shouted something behind her, someone tried to catch her up, to give her back her satchel, but she rushed on head long, without seeing or hearing. She ran all the way to her block, up the staircase to the flat, along the corridor to her room.

Lubka didn't go to school after that. Then she was called there, together with her mother. Then Lubka said to Praskovya that if she beat her to death she would never go to school any more. Praskovya didn't insist. School learning seemed to her a difficult wisdom. She herself had only one year of secondary education. She thought that may be Lubka takes after her and she didn't force her to learn. And thus Lubka's 'learning' came to an end.

From this incident we get a clear picture about Lubka's behaviour. Lubka was not born as a bad girl. Situations made her to get attached with Senka. But when she realized that his intention was not good she avoided him. Because of him she left the school. If her mother compelled her to go to school she might have gone. But there was nobody there to lead her in the right way. She lived according to her wishes. So we can't accuse her.

After leaving school Lubka went to work in the light bulb factory. She had so many friends, both boys and girls at her neighbourhood. In the evening they all came to her house and they enjoyed there till late night. Seeing all these, her neighbours said that she brings men home to her place and spends night with them.

In the Comrades Court many came forward to talk about Lubka. The court got enough facts. Thus Zalomin got much more facts about Lubka's life and Lubka herself than he had before the hearing: the girl had grown up without any guidance or even supervision. Her mother was careless and irresponsible. She had not forced Lubka to continue at school. Those surrounding her, including her co-tenants, were unconcerned and uninvolved, they'd known more than anybody else about the family situation of the Sapozhnikov's but had never intervened to help in any way. Of course, the mother was mainly to blame, but the daughter had become mature and would have to answer for her own actions.

Most of the tenants were of the opinion to remove Lubka from their housing authority area and transfer her to another more remote part of the Soviet Union. Hearing this for the first time Lubka felt afraid and she wanted to cry. The many eyes looking at Lubka were not kind. The pale faces turned towards her were lit by no warmth or sympathy.

The Comrades Court had passed a motion of public censure on Lubka Ivanovna Sapozhnikova for violation of the peace in a communal flat and undignified behaviour. Zalomin gave Lubka a chance to save herself. It had been taken a long argument to win her that chance. Lubka had three months, and the judges were charged with checking the behaviour of Sapozhnikova no later than the date indicated in the minutes.

When the court dispersed Lubka told her mother not to wait her and so Paraskovya went home. Lubka's friends came round her. Mikhail had meant to speak to Lubka but had decided not to. He didn't like that lot around her. So he'd turned and walked briskly away.

That night we can see Lubka thinking about her life. Everything in her life seemed dirty and repulsive to her. She looked at herself as a girl from a new, grown up angle. She thought why her mother let her to leave school. If her mother forced her to go to school she might not have fallen into the bad company and became nuisance to her neighbours. After completing her education she might have got good job and thus her life itself might got changed. From her thought we can assume that Lubka felt regret for stopping her education. If anybody was there to compel her to go to school she might have gone. But nobody was there to give guidance. She was always alone, a daughter of a soldier's widow. Her mother had always told her that her father had died in the war. In her non-questioning way Lubka had not thought which war he had died. But it was clear to her that he couldn't have died in the war as she had born after it. So in her mind a question raised- where was her father. She thought her father was probably some petty thief. So her mother a tramp, her father a good-for-nothing, and she couldn't describe about her home. As for herself, she was beyond contempt, 'a stupid fool'.

Here we can see the tormenting mind of a young girl who didn't even know who her father was. Without getting the true love and care from a cultured family she had become a good for nothing and instead of giving her proper advice, the society also isolated her and considered her a bad girl.

Again when Lubka started going to the factory her mood gets even worse. She worked harder that day than ever before and her usual lethargy vanished. It was then that Lubka discovered that anger creates strength. Returning from the dining room after the lunch Lubka met Mikhail. He stopped her and asked her whether she was fine. Lubka smiled to him and asked him why he ran off the previous day. But Mikhail was embarrassed and he didn't know what he wanted to say.

Lubka's gang lay low for quite a long time. But two weeks later again they got together at lubka's flat. Once again drunkenness and debauchery at Lubka's flat. Lubka had promised to Zalomin that there would be no such things any more but she didn't keep her promise. When her friends came she forgot all the conditions and sang and dances with them. So without thinking the consequences Lubka always gave preference to the pleasure she gets. This is the reason why all her neighbours hate her.

Mikhail and Lubka did not meet again for a long time. They would see each other from far off, nod and hurriedly go on their way. The girls often talked about him, they liked the young fitter. He was a great lad, lively sang well, and he played the guitar. He was handsome, he was a gipsy. That was why he could sing and play the guitar.

Mikhail wanted to talk to Lubka very much; he wanted to know more about her. Sometimes, in passing he would ask Lubka's forewoman about Lubka's behaviour as if it was part of his official duty; after all they had sent him to court for her. The forewoman would answer that Sapozhnikova was steadier and had lost her former slackness, but still showed no perceptible interest in her work.

Mikhail was waiting for a chance to talk with Lubka. At last he told her that he wants to marry her. Mikhail really loves Lubka. He was not like her other boyfriends. In the very first talking itself he proposed her to marry. He loved her truly. That's why he was ready to forget all her bad habits. The following conversation supports this statement.

Without thinking, as you would jump into save a drowning person, Mikhail said: 'Lubka, marry me'. She looked at him, stunned, frightened, and saw his face, also frightened, like a reflection of her own. They were both silent for a minute, transfixed and petrified. He held her hand in his. Her fingers were the first to come to life, she stretched them gently but did not withdraw them completely, as if testing her freedom. Lubka looked at him, narrowing her eyes slightly, she pulled gently on her fingers, but he held her hands harder and would not let them go.

Lubka liked him a lot but didn't want to think about what might happen in the long term. The unexpected proposal, the first in her life, delighted her and she was longing to become his wife.

To make Monday come more quickly Lubka started cleaning her home. She wanted to give everything a thorough cleaning, to change everything round, and to turn her home upside down and inside out. By Sunday evening the only thing left to do was to shine up the fresh polish on the wooden floor. Lubka, in an old cotton housecoat and worn-out slippers, was cleaning a brush full of hairs over a newspaper. It was at this moment that her gang came. But Lubka boldly said that the door will never open for their company.

From Lubka's words it becomes clear that she had changed a lot. Before meeting Mikhail her life was aimless and thoughtless. But when she realised that somebody was there to love and care her, Lubka's attitude towards life changed and she avoided her friends. So her belief in Mikhail's words, that he would marry her prompted her to become a good girl.

At Her Father's and Her Mother's Place

This is a story of a thirteen year old girl from a broken family and her separated parents. Her father and mother were divorced when she was only five years old. She lived with her mother and in her thirteenth year she went to live with her father. Talya liked living with her father. It was a happy, carefree and relaxed life like a continuation of the school holidays.

For Talya, he was a good father. She thought how nice it was there with him and what a shame it was that they didn't all live together. Talya played many games with her father and she enjoyed every minute she spent doing things in the company of her father. Talya felt like this because at her mother's home she was always alone. Her mother was always busy and she never gets time to spend with her. So her father's behaviour gave her childish mind great pleasure. Talya's father was very friendly with her. He enjoyed playing with his little daughter. He knew a lot of poetry by heart and in the evening they read, separately or aloud, together. He drew well and he also readily helps in her studies.

When her father presented her a watch she was overjoyed because in her life it was for the first time she was receiving a gift. Since she and her mother were living alone there was nobody there to give her gifts.

Their happy, carefree life came to an abrupt end. Talya found a letter sent to her father and it was a love letter. A feeling of utter weariness swept over Talya when she understands that her father was in love with a strange woman. Reading that letter she understands that her father's lover was very much annoyed by her arrival and that lady was waiting for her departure. Talya can't endure her sadness and she went back to her mother's house.

Talya's behaviour shows that even though she was a small girl she had a mature state of mind. That's why without even telling about the letter to her father she decided to go back to her mother. She loved her father very much, but after reading the letter her mind had changed. She never expected such a thing from her father. She even hated going with him to her home. He took her home to Pulshik Street by horse cab. Normally she enjoyed the sleigh-ride but that day she sat woodenly, her head lowered, her eyes fixed on the hole in the blanket that covered their feet.

Talya's father's house was well-furnished and everything in

the house looks neat and tidy. But her mother who was financially poorer than her father was always busy and she had no time to arrange things in the house or we can say that she was not interested in that kind of things.

After staying with her father for some days Talya had some changes. Talya thought why everything so horrible at home. The iron stove, the 'bourgsoiska' still stood in the middle of the room exhaling an aroma of lukewarm paraffin although radiators had long providing the heating. An unpainted iron bed along one wall and a wooden bed, with a grey flannel blanket along the other wall, met in one corner. Cups, an empty sugar-bowl, and a plate with some stale bread on it stood on the square, news paper covered table. The curtainless windows looked out on to blind brick walls.

From Talya's thought we can infer that after living with her father she was very much conscious about the poor condition of her house and the food they eat. Since she had a luxurious life with her father, she wishes to lead such a life with her mother as well. That's why she told her mother to re-arrange her house. Even though she went with her father and lived a luxurious life with him she never forgets her mother. Talya loved her mother very much. She was eager to see her. That's why before going to sleep she wrote a letter to her mother, not to leave the next day morning without waking her.

Talya's mother always went to work early in the morning, before Talya was properly awake. Though she was a nurse, she had a lot of other things to do as well, besides her work. Even in her off days she was busy. Talya knew about her mother's work. Talya didn't ask questions about her mother's visitors. It was obvious to her that people needed her mother and that was why her mother gave them all her time. She rarely arrived home before nine or ten in the evening, and then she would have to wash, sew and cook. In her life Talya never accused her mother. As a daughter she always supported her.

Talya didn't tell her mother anything about the letter she read from her father's home. This shows Talya's maturity. She knew that her mother will be tensed hearing about it. So Talya kept it as a secret. But when she got ready to go to school she asked her mother why they were not living with her father. But her mother didn't answer to her question. There existed some reason behind their separation which only her mother and father know.

As a grown up daughter she have the right to know about it. While talking about that matter her eyes became cloudy with tears. This itself shows how distressed she was. If Talya had known the reason behind their separation she might not have been tormented herself that much. But she didn't know anything. She very much yearned to live together with her father and mother.

A Week Like Any Other

A Week Like Any Other tells the story of a working mother and her family. The story was narrated in the diary from, the device being motivated by the assumption that this was material gathered by the narrator for filling in a questionnaire. Almost very event in Olga's day is recorded.

Olga is a typical product of the soviet years, caught between work and the deadening weight of domestic chores on the home front. She was a twenty-six year old urban working wife and mother of two children. Olga was very busy in the morning. But even in her busy life she was very beauty conscious and she hated her features and wants to become more beautiful. Like every women she also wished to become more beautiful but never gets time to spend for it.

Because of her busy life she often forgets to comb her hair. Olga was very busy at home and her husband Dima always tells not to rush like a mad woman. Every morning she would be busy in the kitchen. While preparing food in the kitchen she wakes Dima and her little children. It was very difficult to wake them up. She would gave the children a quick wash and dress them and gave them milk and breakfast. Dima eats a fuller breakfast, but most days she can't eat at all, and have a cup of coffee. At last she would lock the door and walk out. There would be great queue at the bus stop, and the bus usually arrives at the stop fully filled. Only five people from the queue were usually let on. And somehow she would reach the Institute.

Though Olga and Dima were working parents Dima was free at home. Olga alone was responsible to look after the children, doing the household duties and it was also Olga who stands in the queue and buys the things from the department store. At the Institute when they got leisure time one of them goes for the shopping.

During those days it was not easy for them to get home. In the metro it was very rush and with all the bags in the hands it was very difficult for them to stand. Here we can see how much Olga suffers for her family. At the Institute, on the way to home, and even when she reaches home she was very busy. Without even changing her dress she goes to the kitchen and prepares food. They eat a lot. For her it will be the first meal of the day. The children were exhausted by the hot, plentiful food. Their eyes were heavy with sleep. She takes them to the bathroom, plunged into a quick bath and then to bed. By nine they will be fast asleep. Then she would wash the dishes and then the children's clothes. She gets their clothes ready for the morning and at last she takes a bath and get to bed at midnight. She will be asleep in two minutes. Through her sleep she could hear Dima getting into bed, but she can't open her eyes, can't answer his questions, and can't return his kiss. Dima winds up the alarm clock and in a few hours the damned thing would explode again.

This shows that Olga is living for her children and husband. She never gets enough time to take rest. Since she was a working mother she was double-burdened. She had to do the work at her institute and also she had to look after her children and husband. In the Institute also she had lots of problems. She had to finish the experiments within a particular time and to summarise the results and wrote the report. Once she said to her subordinate that she had lost herself, in the pile of work and worry, in the Institute and at home.

Olga was completely fed up with her institute and home. She was a young woman; she also has many desires like, having some secret moments with her husband, going for an outing with her husband and children. But here Olga didn't get enough time to have even a peaceful sleep. Actually this was not only Olga's problems but the whole working mother's problems. A working mother of a nuclear family in any country has to face all these problems. So through this story the writer Baranskaya portrays not only Olga's double-burden life but the whole working mother's problems.

8
KAMALA DAS : A BARD OF LOVE

In India the short fiction had always been popular in the regional languages among women writers. Kerala can boast of a long line of short story women writers in Malayalam. Kamala Das is one of those rare writers who is equally at home both in regional language as well as in English. It is surprising to note that when over a hundred and fifty stories have issued from her pen in Malayalam, Kamala Das has used the short story from very sparingly in English. She is a writer who consistently delves deep inot her consciousness to create female images that are at once herself and the other. Kamala Das' stories are a reproduction of women's speech patterns and throb with the lives of women characters caught in different moods and situations. The stories of Kamala Das arc always about love, lost love and nostalgia. As a woman writer she portrays the feeling of women which are not expressed by ordinary women. The taboos of the society are broken in the writings of Kamala Das.

The Lost Nilambari

In *The Lost Nilambari* Kamala Das depicts the frustrated marital life of Dr. Subhadra Devi. Throughout her life Subhadra never gets a chance to enjoy. From her teenage to the end of her life she lived with a love-lorn heart.

Subhadra was a Malayali girl living in Madurai with her family. Her father was an ophthalmologist in Madurai. Subhadra feels adoration to her music teacher Ramanujan Shasthrigal. Because of her adoration to that Brahmin youth she was adamant about getting her nose pierced and began to grow her hair and wore jasmine garlands on it in the evenings. She gave up frocks and switched over completely to half-sari. She became a vegetarian. Ragas would dance on her lips all the time.

The sudden change in the daughter's behaviour surprised Subhadra's parents but when her father understands about her love her changes became a proof to the father that his daughter was in love with her guru. Thus in order to emancipate Subhadra from that fascination he told Shasthrigal that he was sending her to Madras for higher studies. Thus Subhadra's adoration to Shasthrigal was nip in the bud by her father and she reached Madras for her higher studies. With a lovelorn heart she stayed there. In course of time, she took up medicine and returned home a doctor. Subhadra's marriage was fixed that same year.

Shasthrigal had by then married his niece Jnanam, Subhadra's classmate. That alliance had been decided on by the families the very next day Jnanam was born. Though Subhadra didn't reveal her love to Shasthrigal, in her mind she loved him very much. She wished him to become her's only. That's why she was disgusted to hear Jnanam's and Shasthrigal's bed room secret. She also didn't want others to know about her adoration to Shasthrigal. After her marriage to Chandrashekara Menon she became a reputed doctor. But the memories of Shasthrigal haunted her even after her marriage. She often remembered Shasthrigal singing the Nilambari. Subhadra and Chadrashekara Menon had no children. When they became old they remained alone. In her life Subhadra felt love towards only one person; that was Shasthrigal. Though Subhadra married Chandrashekara Menon the memories of Shasthrigal remained in her heart and she never had any love for her husband. She made love to her husband, with a feeling of numbness lurking in some unknown corner of her heart. Her husband had never aroused her. But without any show of indifference, day and night she fulfilled all her duties as an upper class Hindu wife. So the outsiders always feel that she was a good wife. Hence, their friends and acquaintances hailed Dr. Subhadr Devi and Chandrashekara Menon as an ideal couple.

When Menon, who always cursed patients, himself, fell ill, Subhadra became restless with a sense of regret. She began to feel that she had not done her duty towards him. Though earlier she never showed any love towards him, when he became ill she looked after him with great care. As he lay helpless, stricken with arthritis, he would shed tears silently. The cause of his sorrow was unknown to Subhadra. She would made lemonade herself and pour it into his mouth. Also foment his body all by herself. Till his death she payed great attention to him. Servants and friends who saw Dr. Subhadra nursing her husband praised her wifely virtues.

After Chandrashekara Menon's death Subhadra decided to visit Madurai alone. She arranged her things with a palpitating heart, like a bride leaving for her honeymoon. So it is clear that Subhadra very much wants to see Shasthrigal. Though several years had passed her love for Shasthrigal remained as such in her heart.

After thirty-three years when Subhadra met Shasthrigal from the Madurai Meenakshi temple her mind became the old teenage girl's who went to study music. Though she felt love to Shasthrigal before revealing her love her father had separated them. So after many years when she met him again she wished to sit with him and fearlessly show her love at least once, and rest her face on that chest. But Shasthrigal never liked to taint her image. He told her that each one has his duty to perform and the aim of their life was to do it. He also told her not to bring harm to her husband's reputation and he had to live there and continue nursing his mad wife.

Here Subhadra's humility is noticeable from her teenage itself. When her father sends her to Madras she didn't oppose him. Similarly when her father fixed her marriage she didn't protest. Throughout her life she silently obeyed everybody without telling anybody about her desires. At the end when Subhadra met Shasthrigal she had a lot of expectations but when he told her that each one has his duty to perform she didn't utter a word against him. With great grief in her mind she returned. Since she had no courage to tell her desires to others, in her life she never gets a chance to enjoy. From the teenage to the end of her life she lived with a lovelorn-heart.

The Sandal Trees

The sandal Trees is a story of lesbian relations. The incident of meeting a lesbian girl prompted Kamala Das to write this story. In this Kamala Das shows the tendency to posit lesbianism as loving and satisfactory in contrast to the hetro sexual relationship which in her viewpoint is dull, dominating and abusive. In this story Kamala Das speaks about the infatuation felt for each other by two women Kalyanikutty and Sheela.

The Sandal Trees is a short novel by Kamals Das depicting the unique intimacy between two heroines Dr. Sheela and Dr. Kalyanikutty. Sheela and Kalyanikutty were childhood friends whose relationship raises many questions from the traditional circles. The complex relationship between the two heroines is capable of quashing the conventional values of man-woman relationships. By the analysis of sexual intimacy between Sheela and Kalyanikutty, the writer focuses on the discrepancy in husband and wife relationships and emotional failures. Intimacy between the two friends is fore grounded so that flaws in marital life are pushed to the background.

It was Sheela's family which financed Kalayanikutty's studies. She studied and became a doctor because of their generosity. But when Sheela's father died, she didn't share her grief and didn't weep with her. It was really shocking for Sheela seeing Kalyanikutty showing no emotions at the death of her father. Still Kalyanikutty's disarming smile drew her towards her. It was not possible for Sheela to continue living without Kalyanikutty's friendship. Sheela shared all her secrets with her. But Kalyanikutty hides her thought from her. Kalyanikutty was very shrewd and she played all kinds of tricks to hold Sheela's friendship. She didn't like Sheela developing close relations with other girls.

Sheela and Kalynikutty were unknowingly involved in an unnatural relationship. For ages Sheela was a slave to her throbbing hands and legs. After that she became Kalyanikutty's beloved. The moistness and taste of her mouth became her. The roughness and tenderness of her body became all her. Finally, Sheela's mother who could not find any other way to separate them, married her off to a rich and educated relative. On the wedding eve Kalyanikutty held her tight and proposed to elope. She considered that the man proposed was ugly, plump and twenty-one years elder than Sheela.

After Sheela's marriage she kept comparing her husband with Kalyanikutty; her husband's mouth that smelt beer and Kalyanikutty's mouth that had sweet smell of durva grass. She can't forget the pleasure Kalyanikutty gave her. Sheela and Kalyanikutty joined for medicine. Both of them were in different colleges. As before,

Sheela's family helped for Kalyanikutty's studies. Kalyanikutty always told Sheela that she had resemblances with Sheela's father. But Sheela always said that her father never touched another man's wife. He was a good soul, and a man of firm faith. Later Kalyanikutty got married to Sudhakarn who was also a doctor. She settled down in Sheela's neighbouring city and visits her every now and then. Kalyanikutty was not proud of her husband who was a healthy and handsome young man.

Later Sheela came to know that Kalyanikutty was constantly fighting with Sudhakaran and she was trying to get a divorce. Sheela was not grieved on hearing the news about her ruined marriage. Her marriage had collapsed while Sheela's remained intact, she thought it with pride. While Sudhakaran and Kalyanikutty, two emotionally charged creatures, were messing up their lives through constant quarrels, Sheela and her husband continued to live in perfect amity. Kalyanikutty, who invariably won the first rank in her examinations, could not make her marital life a success. Later on getting a divorce, Kalyani came to see Sheela before going off to Australia. She said that she would get Sheela a job in Australia. But Sheela said that she won't leave her husband and go anywhere. She boarded the plane promising she would come back to India after a year. But she didin't.

Sheela and her husband had no children. Dr. Sheela who helped other women to become mothers' didn't have the good fortune to become a mother. But her husband never showed any grief over it. One day at her clinic Sheela noticed a perfectly healthy, middle-aged woman dressed impeccably in a sophisticated manner. A beauty still retained, though slightly artificially, the glow of youth in her face and her hair. She moved towards Sheela hesitantly. One her lips a half smile, like that of a person halfway through a narrow wooden bridge, lingered tremblingly. Sheela recognised her when only that woman introduced herself that she was her old play mate Kalyanikutty. It was twenty-six years since they last saw each other.

Kalyanikutty moved closer to her and kissed her on her neck and ear. She told her that she had given up her job in Australia and gone to Delhi two years ago and that she was the widow of an Australian. She said that she had returned to see Sudhakaran and to spend a few days and night with him. Sheela replied that Sudhakaran got married and they have a teenage daughter. His wife is under her treatment. Sheela told her not to tempt Sudhakaran because his wife was ill and she won't be able to bear any more grief and their marriage life will be ruined.

Dr. Sheela mentally hated her husband. But she did all her wifely duties perfectly. After his retirement he started calling her Dr. Sheela, before she used to call her 'Sheela' or 'Ammu'. Those days he never asked her about anything that happened at her hospital. But after retirement he started asking questions and that upset her. He had become almost like a diseased limb. A limb that had to be cut off and removed from her. Sitting down to eat with him and lying down on the same bed with him became extremely distressing.

Kalyanikutty often visits Sheela and told her that she wishes to see sudhakaran. Seeing Kalyanikutty's crying face Sheela arranged a meeting with Sudhakaran. They received each other in silence, gazing at each other with thirsty eyes. That night they called a taxi and left together. Kalyanikutty and Sudhakaran had spent a few nights and days together.

When Sheela went to the airport to despatch Kalyanikutty, she told Sheela that after Sheela's father's death her household manager personally handed over to her some money and a letter her father had written. In that letter it was written that Kalyanikutty was his daughter. Though Kalyanikutty left, the memories of her playmate again came to Sheela and she wished for a reunion with her.

There are two themes discussed in this narrative. First one is intimacy between man and woman, second is intimacy between two women. These intimacies though inconsistent in their exposures are Kamala Das' attempts to establish a transparent bond between people.

The Cruel Ring of Truth

This is a story of a widowed mother and her daughter. In this story Kamla Das narrated the miserable plight of a widowed mother. Her only daughter who settles with her husband after marriage avoided her and the mother can't endure her loneliness.

The mother in this story is really an embodiment of tolerance. Her husband had died the year the daughter was born. Since then she had lived her life trying hard to fulfil the obligations of both father and mother. As a woman she also had all sorts of emotions and feelings. But she suppressed all her emotions and lived for her daughter. She feared that a second marriage would badly affect her daughter's future life. Many men had tried to tempt her into sin in the days when her beauty was a burden to her in the absence of a husband. But she had lived, envisioning both god and goddess in her daughter, without walking into anyone's sexual snares.

The mother loved and cared her daughter very much. To conceal from her daughter her middle-class origins, she had borrowed money from her friends, bought her silk clothes, arranged the top teachers of the city for her tuition, and lit coloured bulbs on the branches of trees in the garden on her birthdays. She brought up her without let her know any hardships in life. So the daughter never had any difficulties in her life. Due to her excessive love the mother always supported her daughter without even thinking whether her daughter's actions were right or wrong.

Eventually the mother had given her in marriage to a rich, well-behaved youth. But the mother started eating the bitter fruits of loneliness for the first time in her life when her married daughter grew gradually distant from her. The sudden change in the daughter's behaviour mentally depressed the mother.

With the passage of time the mother grew absolutely lonely. Her hair turned quite grey. She lost her sleep and always thought about her daughter. Her blood pressure went up due to lack of sleep, and her neighbours could view her only with sympathy. The daughter never came to see her and not even phoned her. Though her daughter never came to see her she never hates her. That's why when the neighbour's asked her whether her daughter visits her she told them that she comes at night because both of them were busy during the day. Thus she learnt even to utter lies for her daughter. She told like this because she disliked others abusing her daughter.

The mental state of a widowed mother is shown in this story. She became a widow in her youth itself and she brought up her daughter all alone sacrificing all her happiness. She believed that her daughter and son-in-law would be there with her till death. But unexpectedly, after the daughter's marriage when she began to behave like a stranger all her beliefs utterly collapsed. She had no other blood relations to share her feelings. Nobody was there to help her. In her life she didn't get any sort of happiness. She had sacrificed her whole life for the well-being of her only daughter.

The Mother and Son

This story highlights the contempt of a son for his rustic mother. The middle aged mother lived a lonely life with her son who no longer cared for her. The mother in this story is an ordinary village house wife. She was very simple and open minded. She was not conscious about her dressing and physical appearance. Even though she had many new and beautiful clothes she always wore old clothes. His only son Unni hated his old mother who lost her beauty. He even hated her way of talking and he thought that her style of pronunciation would destroy his dignity before others. Because of this he always avoided her getting acquainted with his friends. For his school anniversary he didn't take her to school.

Unni's father was in Qatar and he and his mother was alone in the house. Unni started hating his mother when he was fifteen years old. Till then he loved his mother and shared all matters with her. The sudden change in his behaviour utterly collapsed his mother. Unni wants her to behave like a modern lady. But she didn't have the habit of going for outings, or for a film or spending the leisure time in engaging other hobbies like reading books or hearing music. She was always busy with cleaning, washing and other household duties. Such manners of his mother made him more disgust.

Unni's mother never liked to become a burden to others. That's why she said she had no fascination to see Qatar when Unni told her to live with father. Father was sending enough money for them and she was not interested to go there and become a burden for him. After saying this, her eyes were filled with tears. From her tears we can infer that she knew that her husband also was not interested in her. So as a wife and also as a mother she failed to get the love which she expected from them.

At the end we can see her unexpected death in an accident. Only after her death Unni understands the value of his mother. Here Kamala Das shows the behaviour of the new generations to their poor parents.

9

THE THEME OF FRUSTRATED WIVES IN THE STORIES OF BOTH KAMALA DAS AND NATALYA BARANSKAYA

We are living in a culture and society which are in no way sympathetic and favourable to women and their minds. This causes a kind of psychic trauma in women. So they are compelled to find out their own way for survival in the male dominated society. They think that these survival strategies they adapt will equip them to cope with the male-centred world. The physical as well as mental torture of women is often unravelled through the effective and powerful medium of literature. A new kind of writing that started in the west at the beginning of 20th century shifted the focus of fiction from the day to day lives of characters to the world of their inner realities.

A woman is admired not for her wisdom but for her elegance. Acumen and intelligence seldom count as qualities of recognition for a woman. Patriarchal ideology curtails woman's autonomy and deforms her personality. Simone de Beauvoir and Kate Millet establish with diverse illustrations that patriarchy, which is sexual politics, operates in life and literature throughout the world. Patriarchy being a social reality, women's reactions to patriarchal oppression or exploitation remain almost identical everywhere. Patriarchal ideology prescribes roles for women which results in a stifling of their individualities. Women seldom transcend the roles; they give up their personal aspirations for the sake of the family. They can create new roles for themselves if they resolve the inner conflict caused by guilt and anxiety of being inadequate mothers and negligent housewives. But this is seldom achieved, as contemporary culture makes women consumers of patriarchal ideology.

The society built on patriarchal values may find the unconventional ideas expressed by women foolish or mad. Natalya Baranskaya and Kamala Das believe that a woman has to wage a double battle; she should resist the external coercion by the patriarchal structures of society on the one hand and the internal dissension produced by members of her own gender on the other. Only her success in this battle can ensure her liberation from the torturous spell of patriarchal culture. The two writers are of the view that the phallocentric organisation of society exerts its vicious influence on women. Patriarchy is an all-pervasive phenomenon in the present-day world. The most dominant spheres of its influences are the family and the domestic life and the institutions of love and marriage. Male cruelty and female subordination are direct consequences of patriarchy. The consideration of motherhood as a redeeming transition from womanhood is a significant aspect of patriarchal thought.

Natalya Baranskaya's and Kamala Das' characters highlight the miserable predicament of woman who struggles to reconcile herself between the society's expectations of womanhood and her own expectation of feminine fulfilment. By analyzing the characters Olga *(A Week Like Any Other)*, Subhadra *(The Lost Nilambari)*, Kalyanikutty and Sheela *(The Sandal Trees)* we can understand that through these characters Baranskaya and Kamala Das underline the psychological aspect of domestic violence and its impact on woman's life.

The characters discussed here are all professionals. Olga a Research Assistant and Subhadra, Kalyanikutty and Sheela were doctors. The character Olga's mind was always tensed. She was over-burdened with her job and household works. Nobody was there to help her at home. She had to do the household tasks and had to take care of the children as well. Olga and her husband Dima were equally educated. But Dima gets enough time to read newspapers, books and for other activities. Olga not even gets time to comb her hair. She also wishes to read newspapers and other books like her husband. But she never gets time for her personal interests.

Both Olga and Dima were employed. But Olga alone was busy with looking after children and household works. Olga was a woman and hence should suffer all atrocities. Men are exempted from these household duties. Though Dima helps her in household works he always gave importance to his personal interests and only after that he helps her. Thinking about her busy life Olga's mind was very much troubled. Her mind was always frustrated with the double-burdened life. Her heart yearns for a hectic-free life. But in order to lead a fully satisfied and peaceful life Olga sacrifices her interests. Thus Olga was a true mother and wife with sincerity and devotion.

The characters Dr. Subhadra, Dr. Kalyanikutty and Dr. Sheela are the victims of marital disharmony. The reason for the incompatibility in their marital relationships is that Subhadra, Kalyanikutty and Sheela were mentally not prepared to accept the person whom their parents proposed as their husbands. Theirs was a lovelorn heart and the reminiscence of their love remained in their heart even after their marriage. A marriage is a union of souls. Both husband and wife should be ready to adjust. The characters discussed here are all women of deep emotions and fine sensitivities who are entrapped in marriages with men who are never cruel, who carry out their husbandly obligations assiduously but are impervious to their wives pleas for understanding, communication and respect for their individuality. Such emotionally incomplete relationship have a fatal effect on the finely tuned female psyche and these women find themselves tortured by a painful sense of loneliness created by themselves to avoid their husbands.

Subhadra and Sheela belonged to the aristocratic family and so they were always conscious about the society. Their mind never wished to bring dishonour to their family. Though they disliked marrying the person whom their parents proposed they never protested. They married them for the sake of their parents. But they were not able to lead a happy life. The memories of their lovers haunted them from the very beginning of their life to the end of their life. They even made love to their husband, with a feeling of numbness lurking in some unknown corner of their heart.

But without any show of indifference, day and night they fulfilled all their duties as an upper class Hindu wife. So the outsiders always feel that they were good wives and hence their friends and acquaintances hailed them as ideal couples.

Here, we can find that Dr. Subhadra's and Dr. Sheela's minds were undergoing great frustration because they never revealed their problems to anybody. They tortured themselves by creating loneliness. Though their husbands love them dearly, they always tried to avoid them by being busy with their patients. Both these characters were unlucky to have children as well. So they were leading a lonely life by all means.

Dr. Kalyanikutty on the other hand married Dr. Sudhakaran who was young and handsome but after the marriage she realised that he was not a husband of her dream. According to her, a husband should offer reverence to his wife. Kalyanikutty was very bold and open minded. She never concealed her problems. She always shared it with her playmate Sheela. She had a very strong mind. She was not at all bothered about the society and other people. She did what she felt the right. When she was fed up with Sudhakaran she aborted his child and went away to Australia and married another man. But after that man's death she again returned to India and restarted her relationship with Sudhakaran. Kalyanikutty lived as per her desires but she never realised the comfort of having peace of mind. She was destined to live glooming like a wandering soul. She also failed to conceive a baby and was the owner of a frustrated mind like Olga, Sheela and Subhadra.

Kalyanikutty was different from Olga, Sheela and Subhadra because she is expressive where as the others are dormant. Kalyanikutty always gave importance to her happiness.

When Kalyanikutty returned from Australia she frequently expressed her desire to meet Sudhakaran. But Sheela told her that Sudhakaran is having a wife and a daughter. His wife is ill and if she go to tempt Sudhakaran their family life will be ruined. But Kalyanikutty is not bothered about Sudhakaran's family life. She is very selfish.

Olga, Sheela and Subhadra were always concerned about the society and they never expressed their wishes. They believed that it was all their fate and lead a frustrated life.

Thus the entire female protagonist discussed in the stories

undergoes psychic pressure such as psychic conflict, confusion, dilemma, struggle, strain, illness and worries due to the impact of various hostile forces with which their mind comes in confrontation. These forces are nothing but problems that a woman has to face in her life like male domination, hypocrisy, the evils of patriarchal social set up, the double standards for the male and the female, male chauvinism, neglect by children, overburden of household duties, dissatisfaction in marriage etc.

10
THE THEME OF SINGLE MOTHERS IN THE STORIES OF BOTH KAMALA DAS AND NATALYA BARANSKAYA

Natalya Baranskaya and Kamala Das by portraying the mind of single parent mothers look at the predicament of women and visualize life for woman as a series of obligations and commitments. In addition to existentialistic reality of life they evoke the sentiment and sensibility of mothers for their role and respect in society.

The mental states of widowed mothers are shown in the stories of Natalya Baranskaya's *The Kiss, Lubka,* and Kamala Das' *The Cruel Ring of Truth.* Psychologically most subtle and most complicated is the life of these mothers. The mother in *The Kiss* and the mother in *The Cruel Ring of Truth* became a widow at the very early age of their life itself. From then onwards they lived for their daughters. As a young woman they also had their own desires to fulfil but they were unlucky to enjoy their life with their husbands. Sacrificing all their happiness they brought up their daughters and married them to rich, well-behaved youths. But after their marriage these daughters became very selfish and they began to behave like strangers to their mothers. This unexpected change of their daughters made the mothers mind very much disturbed and troubled.

The mother in *The Cruel Ring of Truth* can't endure her loneliness. She became depressed and her daily life was badly affected. The reminiscence of her early life came to her mind and that golden memory made her mind more disturbed. Eventually she became sick due to her mental depression. The mother in *The Kiss* was also leading a lonely life. There was nobody to share her feelings. Her daughter never gave priority to her mother. Nadezhda's attempt to indulge more time in her work was also not worthwhile to escape from the stress and strain of loneliness. Later she got acquainted with a young man. Only three times they met but simply sharing time with him made her mind refreshed. She wished for a union with him. But at the end, her obligation towards her daughter forbade her from that and she sacrificed her whole life for her only daughter.

The mother in *Lubka* lived with her husband only for two months. After that the war came and her husband went to the warfront and died there. At that time Praskovya Egorovna was only twenty two years old. Only two months she had known the happiness in her life. Before attaining the maturity to start a marital life she became a widow. Her young mind couldn't endure the sudden demise of her loving husband. There was nobody to share her sadness and lead her in the right path. If she had a child in their relationship she might have endured her sadness and lived for that child. But before they had managed to start a child her husband died.

At the very first days Praskovya was really confined and this often created a fear that she may think negatively of harming herself. But after a while, she appeared with great change in her mentality. Her immature mind was unaware about the right and wrong. She got involved in illicit relations. She had a depressed heart searching for bodily pleasure. One year after her husband's death she became pregnant and gave birth to a daughter. We can't accuse Praskovya, because her loneliness and immaturity forced her to lead such a life. In her youth though Praskovya out of her bodily delights went with many men she never avoided Lubka her only daughter. She didn't marry again. She worked hard and brought up her daughter. So it can be claimed that Praskovya is a loving mother.

The mothers in *The Mother and Son* and *At Her Father's and At Her Mother's Place* were also lonely mothers even though they have husband's. Unni's father was in Qatar and so he and his mother was alone at home. Similarly Talya and her mother were living alone since her mother and father live separately. Unni's mother cares him very much but he hates his plain old fashioned mother. He always ignored her and this made her mind depressed. Though she tried to become more attached to Unni he always avoided her. In his childhood Unni showed great affection to his mother but when he entered to his teenage he started hating his mother. The sudden change in her son's behaviour badly affected the mother's mind. Though her husband sends her money and all other things she wants he also failed to give her the love and care. So as a mother and as a wife she was not getting the love and care which she wished to get.

Since her husband and only son always avoided her, she was astranged at home. Out of her loneliness she was lost in thought and always remained gloomy. She lost interest in everything and one day while crossing the road a bus knocks down her and she met with death. Without fulfilling her desires she died with a frustrated heart.

Talya's mother and father were living separately due to some personal problems. Talya was with her mother. Talya's father was a doctor and her mother an ordinary nurse. Her father was financially sound than her mother. Talya and her mother were dwelling in a small house. Talya's mother never troubled her father seeking assistance though they were living in a pathetic condition compared to her father's. She brought up Talya by making aware of her all the difficulties that different classes of people suffering to sustain their life. She was an ideal mother. By leading a lonely life Talya's mother became very bold and she was a woman of strong determination.

Talya's mother never had a feeling of scorn towards her husband though she was living separately. It is clear from her words. She always tells Talya that her father is a good person and she must love her father. She is living away from her husband due to certain personal problems between them. But in her mind she loved him very much. In order to get out of her loneliness she was always engaged in some works and hence never had time to be wasted off thus worrying. She proved an ideal mother and definitely an ideal woman as well.

So here, except Talya's mother all other mothers are ignored when their children got settled in life. This creates a sense of alienation and emptiness in their mind. Darkness and negligence overpower their psyche. They were abandoned by their children and husbands and so they become an excess in the family.

11

THE THEME OF FAMILY AND FAMILIAL RELATIONS IN THE SELECT STORIES OF KAMALA DAS AND NATALYA BARANSKAYA

Family is the basis of human society. It is the most important primary group in society. It is the first and the most immediate social environment to which a child is exposed. It is an outstanding primary group, because it is in the family that the child develops its basic attitudes.

Although the nature and structure of the family vary from one society to other, a society without families is not known to us. Relationship between the members of the family is deliberately formed basing on marriage and descent. The members are bound to each other by certain code of norms, right and obligations. The interpersonal relationships within the family make the family an endurable social unit. It is the fundamental social group on which the conception of society rests. In simpler societies members of a family are found to reside in the same household but in complex societies, some of the members may live apart under several circumstances.

The family is not only the basic social group; it is also viewed as an oldest institution of mankind, which has the power to withstand social changes. The biological and social reproductions of the family are indispensable for the society to maintain its continuity.

In India people learn the essential themes of cultural life within the bosom of a family. India is traditionally a male-dominated society, where woman's rights are subordinated to group or social role expectations. The joint family is an ancient Indian institution, but it has undergone some changes in the late twentieth century and nuclear families become prominent in India as in the West. There are two types of families, the patriarchal family and the matriarchal family.

Patriarchy is a social system in which the male is the primary authority figure central to social organization. In patriarchal families fathers hold authority over women and children. In a patriarchal society property and title are inherited by the male lineage.

. The matriarchal families are mother dominated. The main significance of this system is that the heirs to the property are women in the family and the men are only allowed to enjoy the benefits during their life time. The son of such community had to use their mother's family name. In the present day world traditional matriarchal societies are very rare though women related laws and issues continue to soar.

Husband - Wife relationship in Select Stories

The great relationship, for humanity, will always be the relation between man and woman. The relation between man and man, woman and woman, parent and child, will always be subsidiary. And the relation between man and woman will change forever, and will be the new central clue to human life.

Indian writers and Russian writers have dealt family relationships with high seriousness because the traditional heritage of India and Russia gives great importance to the family unit. They do not shy away from experimenting with any shade of human experience. They have extensively dealt with the theme of man-woman relationship which has a great historical, sociological and cultural significance.

Literature reflects not only the social reality but also shapes the complex ways in which men and women organise themselves, their interpersonal relationships and their perception of the socio-cultural reality. The attitude of the author towards men and women portrayed by the author in his works and the attitudes of the characters, male and female, to one another highlight gender relationships as well as the author's attitude towards these relationships. The author explores and examines the relationship of man with his fellow men, the social forces at work around him in all their bewildering complexity. This process of examination covers the entire gamut of human experience, the most significant being the man-woman relationship.

From the sociological point of view, the role of husband-wife is the principal component in a family context that has undergone a vital change due to growing enlightenment and the movement for emancipation of women. In this regard, literature has played a sterling role in raising the reader's consciousness. In various forms, it has provided a glimpse into female psyche and dealt with the full range of female experience. It portrays, without inhibitions, the new woman who refuses to play a second fiddle to her husband in various walks of life.

In Baranskaya's *A Week Like Any Other,* she captures the essence of women's tension's about their roles at home and on the job through her character Olga. Olga was a happy married mother of two children and a committed scientist. Olga was a real Soviet mother. Even in her busy life she was not ready to abort her second baby which came unexpectedly. She was bold enough to tell her husband that she was not ready to kill her baby. Though Dima wanted to abort it, later he himself told her to have the baby. So as an ideal husband and wife they were ready to admit each other's desires.

The second baby came and it was a girl and she was so beautiful like Dima. Olga had to leave the factory, where she had only worked for six months. She had stayed at home earlier for a year after Kotka's birth, and nearly lost her diploma because of it. But Dima got a second job, he taught at the technical college in the evening. Since she couldn't manage the two children on her own Kotka had to go to the crèche again and he kept getting sick and spent more time at home then there.

When Kotka started going to the kindergarten Olga joined as a Research Assistant. Then Gulka was sent to the crèche. There was nobody to help them. Olga herself did all the duties. Olga had lost herself in the pile of work and worry, in the institute and at home. Olga alone bore the burden of looking after the children even though both of them are having equal responsibilities in a family life. But, here the educated Olga lost her job and diploma because of her tight schedule. This is not only a problem among Olga and Dima, but in the whole world mothers ought to take the responsibility of looking after children. No father will take leave and look after the children. This is the case in the holidays as well. Fathers have their own hobbies and interests. They wanted to read the news papers and other journals. But the working mother have to do all the household duties as well as taking care of the children. We can take evidences for this from the story. Here we can see after doing all the cleaning, washing and cooking Olga bathing Kotka, then Gulka screamed and crawled into the bathroom, leaving the door open. "Dima, come and get your daughter!" Olga shouted.

"May be I've done enough today? I want to read", Dima replied.

"And I don't"?

"Well, that's up to you, but I have to".

"And I don't I suppose".

While she was carrying Kotka off to the bed Dima was sitting in an armchair reading a journal, he really was sitting and reading. As Olga pass by she said loudly: "Incidentally, I've got a degree as well you know, I'm just as highly trained as you are".

This is the words of a frustrated educated working woman. Olga was also highly educated as her husband. But never gets time to develop her career. Both of them were working but at home Dima gets enough time to read his favourite books and other journals. But Olga alone has the responsibility to look after the children and to do the household duties. Being tired she lost her endurance and retorted to Dima. Dima's behaviour made Olga extremely nasty and hurtful and when the children disobeyed she slapped them.

Olga can't endure her grief and out of this grief she slapped her daughter. She felt very sorry for herself. Olga responded to Dima only because of her fury in that moment. She never hated her family. As a wife and as a mother she was always perfect. She always gave priority to her husband and children. That's why she felt regret after rebuking her children and Dima.

Olga was an ideal wife and mother doing all the duties by herself. Since she was working, she was busy not at home but also at the institute. In her busy life she didn't have time to take her food properly. Like her husband she was also educated but she was a mother and had to look after her children and do all the duties at home. She is a woman who is ready to sacrifice all her desires for the well-being of her husband and children. But when she was over tired doing all the duties by herself she unknowingly retort to her husband. Though Dima provoked her, he loved her very much.

Here both Dima and Olga were equally educated, Dima got a better job but Olga lost her diploma and seniority since she had taken leave for her delivery and to bring up her children. Dima gets enough time to develop his career. Since Olga was an urban working mother she was always busy. In between the work at her institute and at her home she never gets time to read even her favourite books. But Dima always finds time to read books and other kinds of personal interests. Everywhere woman is always sacrificing. Any way no man is ready to sacrifice his pleasures.

Though the wives are having the same qualification and position like their husband the latter ones are always free to enjoy all sorts of freedom. After the office work she alone has the responsibility of looking after the children and carrying out the household works. This is because of the male dominance. In every corner of the world we can see this. We can take evidences for this from the story:

When Olga told Dima that in one year she had taken seventy-eight days leave at her institute, ie; nearly a whole quarter Dima said "well, Olya, may be its better to give up work altogether. You spend nearly half the year at home as it is".

"And you want me to spend all of it here? Anyway, we couldn't possibly live on what you earn. If I didn't have all this to bother about I could probably earn more, 200-220 roubles. And, in actual fact, if you add up all the days you don't get paid, you probably only earn about sixty roubles a month. It's not worth it".

"No, no! Dima', Olga said, 'you want me to do all the routine stuff, while you do your interesting work, because you think my work isn't worth it. You're just a rotten capitalist".

"May be I am', say Dima with an unfriendly smile, 'but it's not just a question of money. It would be better for the children as well. The kindergarten is bad enough, but the crèche is even worse. Gulka hardly gets out at all in the winter, and she's always got a cold".

"Dima, do you really think I don't want what's best for the children? You know I do, but what you're suggesting would kill me. What about my five years at university, my degree, my seniority, my research? It's easy for you to dismiss at all, but if I didn't work I'd go mad. I'd become impossible to live with. Anyway, there's no point in talking about it. There's no way that we could live on your salary and at the moment you really haven't been offered anything else".

"All right, Olya all right! I was wrong to mention it. I just had this vision of a different, ordered kind of life. If I didn't have to fetch the children all the time I could work so much better, I wouldn't feel so constrained. May be I'm being selfish. I don't know. Let's drop it".

Here Dima is a working father and Olga a working mother, but Olga alone has the responsibility to maintain the house. Though women are given equal rights to men, society always entrust the upbringing of children and household duties on women only. This is a universal truth. If any woman tries to violate this she will be considered astrayed by the society.

In Baranskaya's *A Week Like Any Other,* the reason for Olga's frustration was that as a working mother she can't maintain alone all the household duties and her work at the office. We can see another frustrated wife Dr. Subhadra Devi in Kamala Das' *The Lost Nilambari.* The reason for Dr. Subhadra Devi's frustration was an unsuccessful love affair. Subhadra's groom Chandrashekara Menon was selected by her father. Though she married Chandrashekara Menon the memories of her music teacher Ramanuja Shasthrigal, whom she adored remained in her heart. In her mind she always adored Shasthrigal and she never loved Chandrashekara Menon. It is clear from Chandrashekara Menon's and Subhadra's conversation:

"Tell me the truth have you been anybody's lover"? Chandrashekara Menon once asked.

"I was a virgin till I got married".

But there was no sense of pride when Subhadra revealed that truth. Her voice almost hinted her feeling that it was unfortunate she did not lose her virginity. She made love to her husband, with a feeling of numbness lurking in some unknown corner of her heart. But without any show of indifference, day and night she fulfilled all her duties as an upper class Hindu wife. So the outsiders always feel that she was a good wife. Hence their friends and acquaintances hailed Dr. Subhadra Devi and Chandrashekara Menon as an ideal couple.

Though Subhadra never showed any affection to Chandrashekara Menon, he always adorned her. During some nights when they were sleeping, he would greedily savour the fragrance of his beautiful wife's skin and hair, as she slept on. She did not resist his caresses but she was not willing to demonstrate her love. Chandrashekara Menon loved Subhadra very much. But he was not getting back it as he wished. Because of his excessive love to her, he feels angry to those who mingle with her. That's why he not even liked the strangers looking at his wife. Every year both of them used to visit Guruvayoor temple. At that time he would walk towards the temple enveloping Subhadra with his hairy arms in order to keep unnecessary intruders at bay. If, in an effort to reach the sanctum to have a darshan of the deity, a man happened to brush against Subhadra; Menon would shout at them.

Subhadra was always busy with her patients and because of this there aroused a quarrel among them. They have no children. Earlier Menon used to feel sad about not having children but finally he began to see her barrenness as a blessing, because he was of the opinion that she won't get any time to care for children. All the time she has thoughts only about her patients.

When Menon, who always cursed patients, himself, fell ill, Subhadra became restless with a sense of regret. She began to feel that she had not done her duty towards him. Though earlier she never showed any love towards him, when he became ill she looked after him with great care. As he lay helpless, stricken with arthritis, he would shed tears silently. The cause of his sorrow was unknown to Subhadra. She would make lemonade herself and pour it into his mouth. Also foment his body all by herself. Till his death, she paid great attention to him. Servants and friends who saw Dr. Subhadra nursing her husband praised her wifely virtues.

By analyzing Subhadra's and Chandrashekara Menon's relationship we can understand that though there existed a lack of affection between them, as a wife Subhadra had done her duty towards him perfectly. In the same way Chandrashekara Menon also cared Subhadra. So their friends and relatives always hailed them as an ideal couple.

In Kamala Das' *The Sandal Trees* we can find the stories of two frustrated wives, Dr. Sheela and Dr. Kalyanikutty. Since there existed a lesbian relationship among them, after their marriage they were not able to lead a happy life with their husbands.

Dr. Sheela's marital life is exactly similar to Dr. Subhadra's marital life in *The Lost Nilambari*. Since Sheela's parents came to know about her unnatural relationship with Kalyanikutty they married her to a relative who was twenty-one years older than her. He was very rich and educated. Though her mind was not ready to accept him as her husband, she didn't protest. She obeyed her parents and married him.

Even after getting married, Sheela can't forget her girl friend. So her husband could not satisfy her because she loved only her girl friend Kalyanikutty and enjoyed the pleasure which Kalyanikutty gave her. During her honeymoon days itself she started comparing her husband with her playmate Kalyanikutty. When she compared his mouth that smelt of beer, cigarette and onion with Kalyanikutty's, which had the sweet smell of durva grass, he failed. However hard she tried, she could not forget the way Kalyanikutty caressed her, pressed her fingers hard into her and satisfied her with her lips, all with the intention of giving her pleasure.

Though Sheela can't truly love her husband she never showed any hatred towards him. Belonging to an aristocratic family she performed all the duties to her husband with great care. But they had no children. Dr. Sheela who helped other women to become mothers didn't have the good fortune to get a child. But her husband never showed any grief over it.

When Sheela's husband was working in the government service he talked less to her and his behaviour made her very silent and there were not much communication between them. Hence, there grows a silence between the husband and wife. Gradually she got used to that silence and it grew between them like a sandal tree, giving her much happiness. But later, after his retirement when he started talking by asking her several questions about her hospital and patients, she got irritated.

In the middle age when their youthful charm fades away Sheela could not resist her hatred for her husband. She felt that he was a limb that had to be cut off and removed from her. She knew that he wouldn't be prepared for a divorce. And she too found it difficult to file a complaint against him in court because he had never physically assaulted her or committed adultery. The fact that he used to embrace her couldn't be presented as a crime. Excess of love is not illegal. Nor is the expression of love a crime.

Sheela knew that she would become free if he would turn angry or beat her at least once. She had made many attempts to provoke him. Once she invited her colleague to her house and sat close to him. All her attempts to provoke him turned futile. He was preparing for a spiritual surrender.

From Sheela's behaviour, it is clear that she was creating a reason to quarrel by provoking him. She wants to avoid him by any means. But her husband out of his maturity never provoked at her behaviour. He was twenty-one years older than her and so he was always ready to forgive her considering her as a small child. But one day he was hurt very much when she told him that he must cut back on his expenses. Already there aroused a complex in him after his retirement and when Sheela told him like that he really became very dull. We can read his mind from the below conversation.

Sheela told him, "it was I who bore the household expenses; you must cut back on your expenses. I have to make all the money myself. Don't forget it".

After this talk he didn't renew his membership at the club. That day when she came back in the evening, she saw him sitting in the garden in a cane chair, with a woollen shawl round his neck.

"Why you didn't go to the club today?" She asked.

"No, I didn't renew my membership. Why should I go? My tennis isn't all that great. It's meaningless going on playing in the hope that my game will improve. It's time I gave up all kinds of ambition".

"Then how will you spend your time? Won't you feel bored? How about reading? I'll pick up a few books from the library. Would you like to read Krishnamurti".

"Why should I read Krishnamurti? Such books don't give me pleasure. I need only ordinary books of fiction. Crime fiction".

Sheela hated her husband's physical features. She even felt that it was to humiliate her that he would not wash his teeth clean and protect them. Her hatred to him was something which he had deliberately created in her. She did attempts at cheating him, at renouncing her chastity. But she saw her husband in every man who came close to her and seeing him there she would back out. And with a shock she slips back into her chastity. She continued to perform her wifely duties. Sitting down to eat with him and lying down on the same bed with him became extremely distressing. As they spoke, the words were like corpses that slid out of their shelves in the morgue. She deliberately slid back to silence, which she would awaken them both, but of no use. Sheela knew how the intensity of hatred became unbearable, for her life without love is terrible. It is better to separate than to lead a life without love. The main reason for Sheeela's disgust to her husband was the age difference between them. Though they never quarrelled among themselves but between them there was blankness and she experiences total estrangement from herself and her surroundings as well. Her disgust to him is clear from this conversation:

Once Sheela's husband asked her, "Dr. Sheela, did you never wish to become a good wife?"

She layed there saying nothing.

"Why don't you answer my question, Dr. Sheela?" he asked.

"You are twenty-one years older than me", I could never see you as my husband", she said.

Sheela also wished to divorce her husband as her playmate Kalyanikutty did when there arouse trouble in their married life. But in front of others Sheela was a dutiful wife that's why she told him it was sure that they would be selected as the ideal couple by the Rotary club.

Sheela had a strong belief that though she hates her husband he always loved her very much and was true to her. But when she came to knew from Kalyanikutty that he was not true to her, at first she can't believe it. She never expected such type of behaviour from her husband. She always believed that he married her because of his eternal love towards her. But hearing Kalyanikutty's words her egoism had completely collapsed. After some moment she felt as though she had been freed from the mental conflicts and the sense of guilt that had been plagued her for years. This is because till then she thought that her husband was true to her even though she hates him.

We can understand Sheela's mental conflict while hearing about her husband's bad behaviour from this conversation between Sheela and Kalyanikutty:

"My husband needs me. He certainly loves me"' Sheela said.

"Him – your old antiquated him! Well, if he loves you so much, why did he spend the whole afternoon in my hotel room yesterday? The fool spent four hours in my room, pleading for my love! I didn't kick the fellow out only because he happens to be your husband". Replied Kalyanikutty.

"Oh, Kalyanikutty, please don't cook up such stories. God will punish you. My husband who has never even looked at another woman – how can he love you? Who will believe this story?" Sheela asked.

"I've never seen anyone more stupid than you, Sheela. He has never loved you. By marrying you he acquired certain respectability in this society. And that day he decided to pretend to be gentle and respectable. It's not just you that his pretensions fooled. It fooled every important person in this city. One look – and I saw the base desires in the depths of his heart. He knew it, so the poor fellow wanted to put an end to his pretensions and spend some time with me. But I don't need such men. They are all vulgar beasts, Sheela".

The memories of Kalyanikutty still remained in Sheela and she wished for a reunion even though she had become old. From Sheela's husband's words it is clear that he was aware of the intimacy between Sheela and Kalyanikutty.

"I realized that you were comparing every past display of love on my part with hers. I was somebody who had reached you after her. I was a mere drizzling arriving hesitantly, timidly, after a full storm".

Sheela's husband realised her relationship with Kalyanikutty at the very first days of their married life itself. He came to know that Sheela was not satisfied in him and felt no interest in his love-making. In her mind there remained always the reminiscence of the pleasure which Kalyanikutty gave her. But she came to know her husband's knowledge about their relationship only after some thirty years after their marriage. Though at that very moment, Sheela felt ashamed to look at his face, she had a great relief welling up inside.

So by analyzing the relationship between Sheela and her husband we can understand that till the end of her life Sheela remained as a frustrated wife because of her love towards her playmate Kalyanikutty.

The family life of Sheela's playmate Kalyanikutty also proved a failure. Kalyanikutty got married to Dr. Sudhakaran. Sudhakaran was a healthy and handsome young man. But Kalyanikutty was not proud of her husband.

Though Kalyanikutty married sudhakaran she was not able to love him. Something blocked her mind in accepting him as her husband. That's why she aborted his child. When Kalyanikutty approached Sheela for an abortion she was not ready to abort. Kalyanikutty didn't want to hear Sheela's words and she told her that she wish to give birth only to Sheela's child. From her words we can assume that even though she married Sudhakaran, in her mind she always loved Sheela and urges for a bodily reunion with her. Kalyanikutty's hatred in giving birth to Sudhakaran's child can be evident from the below conversation:

"I don't want to give birth to Sudhakaran's child. A feeling that my womb has been polluted nags at me. I've never had any respect for Sudhakaran. I'm not prepared to carry in my body for ten months the child of an ordinary man like him. I'll never give birth to his child".

Kalyanikutty was very bold and her decision was very strong. That's why when Sheela was not ready to abort the child without even saying good bye to her Kalyanikutty walked out and left her. She never listened to others' words and always did what she thinks right.

Sudhakaran was not a husband of Kalyanikutty's dream. According to her a husband must respect his wife. She wants her husband to be decent like Sheela's husband. Though Sudhakaran was young and handsome he didn't know to behave properly. Kalyanikutty wished to get a husband who is well-mannered. Her desire is evident from her words:

She told Sheela: "I always felt jealous of you. Even when you accepted a man twenty years older than you as your husband, I felt jealous. Because your husband was not someone like my Sudhakaran. Whenever I saw your husband sitting in the veranda wearing a blue dressing gown and reading a newspaper, I used to envy your good fortune. My Sudhakaran was young and manly. But somehow his frustrations made a beast out of him. He never knew the golden rules of behaviour or etiquette. I hesitated in introducing him to a company of gentlemen. He used to call me 'you woman', 'slut' and so on. He had no respect for me. So I left him and went away in search of a husband who could respect me".

Later on getting a divorce Kalyanikutty went to Australia. While going she promised Sheela that she would come back to India after a year. But she didn't. After a long period when Kalyanikutty came to see Sheela, she had a lot of changes. She had become very young. She told Sheela that she was the widow of an Australian – a rich and happy widow.

Kalyanikutty had come back in order to have a reunion with Sudhakaran. Once Kalyanikutty had ruined Sudhakaran's life by divorcing him without any reason. When Sudhakaran started to live a happy life with his second wife and daughter again Kalyanikutty was trying to ruin his life by tempting him. Kalyanikutty was not at all conscious about others grief. She only gave importance to her happiness and was ready to do anything to fulfil her desires. In order to show Kalyanikutty's selfish mind and her desire to live again with Sudhakaran, we can take evidences from the story:

When Sheela asked her why she came to India Kalyanikutty said: "Till now I haven't asked myself why I'm coming back. I'm not here to inform my folks who are still alive that I, who started life as a poor girl, am now rich and successful. Nor am I here to make you feel jealous. Perhaps, I'd like to see Sudhakaran again. To spend a few days and nights with him...tell me, Sheela, is he still around? Has he married again? Does he remember me?"

Kalyanikutty's words prove that she possesses strange intimacy with her former husband. Sudhakaran and Kalyanikutty met again and spent few nights and days together. After thirty-three years they again had a honeymoon. Kalyanikutty was trying to abduct Sudhakaran and his daughter from his second wife who is very simple. Though Sheela told her about the pathetic condition of Sudhakaran's second wife, Kalyanikutty was not ready to retreat from her decision. She was very merciless that's why when, Sheela told her about Ammini's mother's situation she told her that she didn't like anyone unnecessarily interfering in her private life. It's clear that she was not taking Ammini to love her as a daughter but her intention was to make a lesbian relationship with Ammini. That's why she told Sheela that her relationship with Ammini will be much stronger than any marriage. The conversation given below between Sheela and Kalyanikutty stands as a proof for Kalyanikutty's heartless behaviour:

Kalyanikutty told sheela, "You'd better not interfere in such things. I don't like anyone unnecessarily interfering in my private life.

"Is Ammini your private life?"

"Ammini adores me. She would like to live with me. And I can make her wish come true."

"But Ammini is only nineteen years old. As a doctor who is treating her mother, I can tell you that taking Ammini away from her mother is not right. That woman can't live without her daughter".

"What will she do when Ammini gets married and leaves her? My relationship with her will be much stronger than any marriage?"

"I don't wish to say anything more about this. You're trying to spoil her".

At the end when Kalyanikutty was going back, there was neither Sudhakaran nor Ammini with her. When all arrangements were made, Ammini's mother attempted suicide. Kalyanikutty cancelled the trip of Ammini when the latter was informed of the suicide incident by Sudhakaran over phone. Hence, Kalyanikutty left alone to Australia. Though married two persons, in her life Kalyanikuttty was alone. She didn't have children and was not able to lead a happy life. The rest of her life she lived as a widow, a rich widow of an Australian.

Depiction of Platonic Love in Select Stories

In Kamala Das' *The Lost Nilambari* we can find a silent love between Shasthrigal and Subhadra. She never revealed her love though she had a sort of infatuation towards him. But by seeing the sudden changes in her behaviour it can be assumed that Subhadra was attracted to Shasthrigal. Subhadra who would never take food without fried fish became a vegetarian. She gave up frocks and switched over completely to half-sari. She was adamant about getting her nose pierced and began grow her hair and wear jasmine garland on it in the evenings. Ragas would dance on her lips all the time.

Subhadra's father had assumed that the music teacher was an old man. But when he happened to see him, the youth sitting before him seemed a hero emerging from the ancient epics. He immediately recalled the changes in her. The sudden change in the daughter's behaviour surprised the parents but after seeing the young handsome Shasthrigal her father understands that his daughter was in love with her guru. The tender and innocent sixteen year-old girl may have become her teacher's slave. He may have charmed her. Thus in order to emancipate Subhadra from that fascination he told Shasthrigal that he was sending her to Madras for higher studies.

Thus Subhadra's adoration to Shasthrigal was nipped in the bud by her father and she reached Madras for her higher studies. With a lovelorn heart she stayed there. In course of time, she took up medicine and returned home as a doctor. Subhadra's marriage was fixed that same year. Shasthrigal had by then married his niece Jnanam. That alliance had been decided on by the families the very next day Jnanam was born.

Though Subhadra didn't reveal her love to Shasthrigal, in her mind she loved him very much. She wished him to become her only. That's why she was disgusted to hear Jnanam's and Shasthrigal's bed room secret. She also didn't want others to know about her adoration to Shasthrigal. We can take evidences from the story to clear this:

'I'm not interested in your secrets," she told Jnanam.

"You're jealous of me, aren't you? I know that you are interested in him".

"What sinful lies you utter! I have felt only a disciple's devotion and respect towards Shasthrigal", Subhadra retorted.

Jnanam broke into a loud pearl of laughter.

"Don't I know your devotion and respect? When he rescued you from the pond, I saw how tightly you held him. It is not possible for anyone, who is almost dead by drowning, to hold her saviour so tightly".

"Don't spread scandals. My marriage has been fixed". Subhadra muttered.

After Subhadra's marriage to Chandrashekara Menon she became a reputed doctor. But the memories of Shasthrigal haunted her even after her marriage. She often remembered Shasthrigal singing the Nilambari. Subhadra and Chadrashekara Menon had no children. They struggled with loneliness even in the old age.

Subhadra was always fond of seeing Shasthrigal. Though several years had passed her love for Shasthrigal remained as such in her heart. That's why after Chandrashekara Menon's death Subhadra decided to visit Madurai alone. Her patients and relatives were alarmed and they tried to stop her when they learnt that she would be driving all the way herself. But Subhadra very much wanted to be on her own. She openly confessed that what she sought was solitude and silence. She had adopted a dress style that suited a widow. But for her trip to Madurai, she packed dark silk sarees in her box. She also kept perfumes, stone necklaces, and red stone ornaments in her box. She arranged her things with a palpitating heart, like a bride leaving for her honeymoon.

Thirty three years had passed and Dr. Subhadra Devi, the eminent surgeon, was back in Madurai in search of something she had lost. But if someone were to ask her what it was that she missed, she would have failed to give a satisfactory reply. Sometimes she had made this trip in order to relive the pain she had endured there the past or to taste the sweetness of that ache she had undertaken such a long journey by car, all alone, without even her driver.

But Subhara who had reached Madhurai to see Shasthrigal was utterly disappointed. Because Shasthrigal's wife Jnanam who was abnormal, told Subhadra that Shasthrigal had died a year before. She had been longing to hear him sing the Neelambari at least once and had lived in hope. But hearing Jnanam's words she was utterly collapsed.

Subhadra wished to leave Madurai the very next day and before going she went to the Madurai Meenakshi temple. Unexpectedly she met Ramanujan Shasthrigal there and she was surprised to see him because Jnanam told her that he died a year before.

Here we can see that the love between Subhadra and Shasthrigal was of a peculiar type. The peculiarity is nothing but the love that had perished before blossoming. Though they feel love to each other, they never revealed it. Fate was against them and they were separated. Shasthrigal married his niece Jnanam and Dr. Subhadra Devi married Chandrashekara Menon. Even after her marriage the memories of Shasthrigal haunted Subhadra. Both Shasthrigal and Subhadra failed to lead a happy married life. Both of them were unlucky to have children also. When Subhadra met Shasthrigal after the long thirty three years she very much wanted to sit with him and tell him of the emotions she had kept hidden in these years. But Shasthrigal never liked to taint her image. He always behaved with maturity. He never tried to abduct the things which he didn't deserve to get.

Even when Subhadra wept inside the car Shasthrigal didn't lose his softness. He told her "I don't wish to taint your image. Each one has his duty to perform. The aim of our life is to do it. You shouldn't bring harm to your husband's reputation. I should live here and continue to nurse my mad wife. There is no other way destined for us".

From Shasthrigal's words it is amply clear that Shasthrigal was not a covetous person. Understanding his limitations he never longed for anything in his life. Even though his wife always quarrelled with him saying about Subhadra he never hated his wife. He believed that all happened because of destiny and lived to nurse his mad wife by teaching music to children.

Here Subhadra's humility is noticeable from her teenage itself. When her father sends her to Madras she didn't oppose him. Similarly when her father fixed her marriage she didn't protest. Throughout her life she silently obeyed everybody without disclosing her desires. Though her husband always criticised her for her lack of affection, he once told to her, "You have all the features of Draupadi. But what attracted me most was your humility".

At the end when Subhadra met Shasthrigal she had a lot of expectations but when he told her that each one has his duty to perform she didn't utter a word against him. With great grief in her mind she returned. Since she had no courage to tell her desires to others, in her life she never gets a chance to enjoy. From the teenage to the end of her life she lived with a lovelorn heart.

So by analyzing this story we can conclude that the love between Shasthrigal and Subhadra was purely platonic.

Depiction of Same-Sex Love in Select Stories

The intimacy between man and woman is marginalized in *The Sandal Trees* to show natural love. In this story Kamala Das shows the infatuation felt for each other by two women, Dr. Kalyanikutty and Dr. Sheela. They were childhood friends and without their being aware of it had taken a strong fascination for each other. The complex relationship between the heroines is capable of quashing the conventional values of man-woman relationships.

Sheela was not possible to live without Kalyanikutty's friendship. She had shared all her secret with her. But Kalyanikutty hid her thoughts from her. When she smiled, Sheeela felt that the smile didn't emerge from any happiness. And that her tears were not rooted in grief. Kalyanikutty didn't like Sheela developing close relations with other girls. Whenever Sheela grew close to classmate, she would start saying all kinds of bad things about that girl. She had a special talent for breaking up relationships. She loved Sheela and wanted her to be always with her. That's why she hated Sheela having close relations with other girls. From the below conversation we can find there is something unusual in Kalyanikutty's behaviour to Sheela.

Kalyanikutty said: "Sheela, if you were a boy you could've now begun to love. My father has taught you. So I'm the daughter of your teacher. Haven't you heard about the princess who fell in love with their teachers daughters? Why weren't you born a boy?"

In the story Sheela admits how much she used to enjoy the caressing and kissing made by Kalyanikutty while they were young. She narrates an incident at the swimming pond:

Sheela said, "Kalyanikutty hugged me tight and started kissing me on my face, my neck and between my breasts. She was panting and tiny drops of sweat appeared over her upper lip. Using all her strength, she pushed me down on the floor of the pond-house daubed with cow dung. Then, sending a deep thrill down my spine, she covered every inch of my body with kisses that really hurt. I shut my eyes in shame and humiliation. I don't remember how long I lay there like a living corpse under her assault. For ages I was a slave to her throbbing hands and legs. After that I became her beloved. The moistness and taste of her mouth became mine. The roughness and tenderness of her body became all mine.

Sheela's mother came to know about the relationship between Sheela and Kalyanikutty. Finally her mother, who could not find any other way to separate them, married Sheela off to a rich and educated relative. Kalyanikutty was ready to live with Sheela out of her mad love and interests in the bodily delights with her. Because of the haughtiness of the youth Kalyanikutty was not at all conscious about the society. She was thinking only about the pleasure she was going to get when together with Sheela. Sheela on the other hand, born in an aristocratic family always feared the society. Though the situation forced her to fall in an unnatural relationship with Kalyanikutty she was ready to rectify it. She was not ready to bring dishonour to her family. That's why she married her relative who was twenty-one years older than her.

At the very first days of her marriage itself Sheela started comparing the two; her husband's mouth that smelt beer and Kalyanikutty's mouth that had sweet smell of Durva grass. The intimacy between Sheela and Kalyanikutty forces the intensity of human relationships that goes beyond physical attraction. The intimacy between Sheela and Kalyanikutty is aptly expressed in the words of Sheela's husband:

"I realised that you were comparing every past display of love on my part with hers. I was somebody who had reached you after her. I was a mere drizzling arriving hesitantly, timidly, after a full storm."

Later Kalyanikutty got married to Dr. Sudhakaran. But she was not able to love him that's why she decided to abort his child. Kamala Das' illustration of intimacy between the friends reaches its zenith when Kalyanikutty says that she prefers to carry the child of Sheela in her womb.

"I don't want to give birth to Sudhakaran's child. A feeling that my womb has been polluted nags at me". Kalyanikutty said.

"Suddenly she sat up and kissed me on my lips. The peculiar smell of her skin conquered me – a sweet smell that reminded me of fresh rain".

"I wish to give birth only to your child" said Kalyanikutty.

Here Kalyanikutty's role of the masculine initiator suffers a set back and she steps back into feminine role when she says she wishes to carry the baby of Sheela in her womb. Kalyanikutty's changing role of gender sheds light into the inconsistency in locating her identity as a woman.

When Kalyanikutty dialled Sheela when she was in danger, she was damn sure of Sheela's arrival at the earliest. Sheela on the other hand reached there in a hurry to save Kalyanikutty's life. When Sheela examined her she learned that it was an uncompleted abortion. If Sheela hadn't reached there at time, Kalyanikutty would have been in danger. Sheela took Kalyanikutty to her home. Though Sheela's husband forbids her, she nursed her childhood friend with great care. To avoid a quarrel between Kalyanikutty and Sudhakaran, Sheela didn't tell Sudhakaran the truth that Kalyanikutty knowingly aborted his child. So it is clear that Sheela always stood for Kalyanikutty's goodness.

In this story the husbands create meaninglessness in the lives of Kalyanikutty and Sheela. Kalyanikutty finds impossible to love her husband Sudhakaran. She cherishes that noble seat for Sheela. Kalyanikutty quarrels with Sudhakaran and gets a divorce and leaves for Australia. Before leaving she invites Sheela to accompany her and she promises to look after her. She has a double purpose in inviting her. One is to possess Sheela; the other to free her from her old husband.

Though Sheela was disgusted living with her old husband she never expressed it before anyone. Belonging to an aristocratic family she always kept her nobility. Concealing her own desires she pretended as an ideal wife. That's why she told Kalyanikutty that she loves her husband and won't leave him. But Kalyanikutty understands that Sheela's marital life was not happy. We can take evidences for this from the story:

"Sheela, you're repeating untruths over and over. And you end up believing your own lies. You don't dare be yourself. You've never been bold enough to admit that you love me. You too know that you'll get rest and peace and happiness only when you live with me. Still you choose for yourself the traditional path. The path to decadence. You pretended that you liked your ugly husband and his bed and his decadent words. And now you have no one to call your own. No one who cares for you. Of course, certain people need you to amputate suppurated diabetic limbs or to do a caesarean and pull out a baby. Who else needs you today?" Kalyanikutty asked.

After a long twenty-six years when Kalyanikutty came back from Australia Sheela couldn't recognise her. Sheeela could not be accused for it because Kalyanikutty had changed a lot. She became very young; no one could say they were of the same age. But in one thing she had no change; her love for Sheela. She kissed Sheela as before she had done. So, even after many years the relationship they had in their teenage still remained in their heart. The main reason for this was that both of them had no children. We know that Kalyanikutty went in search of another husband because she didn't like Sudhakaran's behaviour. Her second husband was decent and very rich but he also was not a husband in her dream. After marrying her, he behaved like he was in possession of a valued thing but in their bed he was a failure. So in her bed Kalyanikutty always cherished only Sudhakaran and her playmate Sheela. That's why after her second husband's death she came back in search of them.

At the end when Kalyanikutty was going back to Australia, at the airport she revealed the most important secret in her life to Sheela. Kalyanikutty told Sheela that what she suspected and told to Sheela many times during her child hood was true. She was not the daughter of Shekaran Master, her real father was Sheela's father. Sometimess her adoration to Sheela forbade her in telling that to Sheela earlier. Any way Kalyanikutty never tried to prove her identity. The conversation given below supports this point.

"I've always known that there is a resemblance. But the reason behind it – I knew it only after your father's death". Kalyanikutty said.

"What are you insinuating?" Sheela asked, embarrassed.

"After your father died, your household manager personally handed over to me some money and a letter your father had written. At that moment I started hating - intensely hating – that man who would never admit that he was my father".

"I can't believe this. My father and mother had lived together so happily, with so much understanding. How can I ever believe my father had betrayed her?" Sheela asked.

"I've kept that letter safely. If you want I'll send you a copy by post. Even knowing you were my sister, I couldn't control myself. I've adored you so much Sheela. I've never loved anyone else like this".

Kamala Das is replaying the oedipal myth in the characters of Sheela and Kalyanikutty, by their unique intimacy in a different situation, ie; amorous love interacting between sisters. The letter she claims to have been written by Sheela's father before his death reveals that they are the children of the same father. Psychologically this relationship may even cause death in one of the characters or both when the truth is revealed.

At the airport Kalyanikutty was cold towards Sheela when she bids goodbye, but Sheela still yearns for her intimacy and physical closeness.

"Kalyanikutty stood up. I expected her to kiss me as in the past. But she just smiled. When I could no longer see her, I stepped out of the airport with a sense of loss. I felt my legs weakening out of sheer exhaustion. I was reluctant to go back to that all-too-familiar world of mine that comprised of my house, the lovely objects on display there, my aged husband, my patients, everything. But there is no other place for me to live, I told myself, and no one else to love me, is there?"

The role of the initiator of intimacy gets exchanged at this time. The timidity of Sheela breaks all fetters and opens up her real self before reality of losing Kalyanikutty. Sheela's intimacy to Kalyanikutty is aptly expressed from her words after Kalyanikutty's departure to Australia.

"I was transformed into a young lass who embraced her girlfriend and sought the blissful rapture of her kiss. A girl who found heavenly pleasures in the bodily touch of her beloved – her beloved who, having swum and bathed in the pond for hours together, smelt and tasted of weeds and mosses, water lilies and medicinal herbs. Oh, my love, how can I live now"? Sheela whispered to the darkness that slowly spread in the car.

These intimacies though inconsistent in their exposures are Kamala Das' attempts to establish a transparent bond between people. Though frowned upon as unnatural intimacy, the relationship between Sheela and Kalyanikutty emerges as a search for truth.

Disharmony in Marriage: A Comparative Study of Olga, Subhadra, Sheela and Kalyanikutty

The wives' in the stories of both Natalya Baranskaya and Kamala Das are frustrated. The intimacy between the couples emits hatred, anger and slavery. Women who longs for individual freedom become a prey to this inevitable bondage. Olga, Subhadra and Sheela transform these negative elements into self-made silence. But Kalyanikutty expresses the same feeling by being outspoken. She breaks the chain of relationship with man and again longs to connect it later. Kalyanikutty is expressive where as Olga, Subhadra and Sheela are dormant. But all of them are having the same motive; freedom from bondage.

In Baranskaya's *A Week Like Any Other* the reason for Olga's frustration was that she had lost herself in the pile of work and worry, in the Institute and at home and even though she was highly educated she failed to get a good job according to her qualification. But the wives in Kamala Das' *The Lost Nilambari* and *The Sandal Trees* lead a frustrated marital life because they had an unsuccessful love affair before their marriage.

Olga was a typical soviet professional woman, a young scientist frantically coping with the double burden of job and family and the soviet exigencies of long commutes, overcrowded facilities, and scarce consumer goods. The urban working mother Olga always gave first preference to her children and husband, but she was always very busy. After reaching home in the evening she had to look after her children and to do the entire household works by herself. Nobody was there to help her. She never gets time to spend for her personal matters. Like her husband she also wishes to spend her leisure time in reading newspapers and other books. But because of the issue of double burden not even once did she get time to read a book or a news paper. Every night she used to go to bed at twelve o' clock and falls asleep as soon she lay on the bed as she was very much tired. Because of this she was not able to respond to her husband's kisses and caressing. Hence they had rare sexual discourse.

Olga was efficient at work, supportive at home, and yet she had many problems. Olga had to bear the sufferings of household duties and looking after kids, even though she had a very supportive and loving husband. She never had known the taste of enjoyment as she had a very hectic schedule. This is a fact to be admitted by every respect. Through a deep analysis we can find that in order to get out of her frustration Olga also longs nostalgically for a world in which time stands still.

By analyzing Kamala Das' characters Dr. Subhadra in *The Lost Nilambari* and Dr. Sheela and Dr. Kalyanikutty in *The Sandal Trees* we can find that Dr. Subhadra and Dr. Sheela were almost having the same characteristics but Dr. Kalyanikutty was a little bit different from them. Subahdra, Sheela and Kalyanikutty had a love affair before their marriage. Though Subhadra's adoration to Shasthrigal was nip in the bud in her mind she always adorned Shasthrigal. Similarly Sheela and Kalyanikutty adorned themselves since there existed a lesbian relationship between them. Both Sheeela's and Subhadra's bridegrooms were selected by their parents. Even though their mind was not ready to accept them as their husband they didn't protest. They had no courage to reveal their desires and they obeyed their parents. Both of them belonged to the aristocratic family and they never wanted to bring dishonour to their family.

Kalyanikutty on the other hand always showed the courage to express her opinion before others. She conducted an abortion on herself just because she was not prepared to carry the child of an ordinary man like her husband. Instead she revealed her desire to conceive Sheela's child which of course is impossible. Subhadra and Sheela born in an aristocratic family always tried to confirm the expectations of the society and pretended to be leading a happy life with their husband. But Kalyanikutty rebels against all conventional norms of marriage and divorces her husband Sudhakaran on learning that she does not love him or like him.

Subhadra and Sheela without any show of indifference, day and night they fulfilled all their duties as an upper class Hindu wife. Hence their friends and relatives considered them as ideal couples. But the memories of their lover always haunted them and they failed to find any charm or rapture in their husbands.

Kamala Das' heroines Subhadra, Sheela and Kalyanikutty even though married failed to have children. The life of these married women becomes sterile without children. They were victims of arranged marriages, they lead their lives indifferently.

The Theme of Maternity in Select Stories

To a traditional woman, matrimony is incomplete without motherhood. Motherhood is regarded as the 'biological destiny' and the greatest ambition of a woman. A child is considered to be woman's happiness and her justification, through which she is supposed to find self-fulfilment and self-realization. Motherhood has always held a very high position in all society. The mother, as a matter of fact, enjoys a higher position of honour than the father himself. A Sanyasi need not stand up to pay his respect to his father. But he must do so if his mother pays a visit to him.

In Natalya Baranskaya's *Kiss* she shows the loneliness of a widowed mother after the only daughter's marriage. Nadezhda Mikhailovna, the senior scholar at the Institute of the USSR Academy of Sciences, was a widowed mother. At the very early years of her married life itself she lost her husband and she lived for her only daughter Natasha. As a young woman she also had many desires. But she never thought about another marriage and never got engaged with other men. Doing her job she brought up her daughter fulfilling all her wishes.

Nadezhda lived in the belief that her daughter will be there to take care in all her needs. But after Natasha's marriage she gave less importance to her mother. She rarely came to see her mother. Thus Nadezhda became alone in her one room apartment. After her daughter gave birth to a child she became much more selfish. Hence, Nadezhda failed to get the love and care which a mother desires to get during her old age.

In order to get out of her loneliness she got acquainted to Viktor, a young man. When Viktor phoned and told her that he will come the next day evening to her home she became enthusiastic. The below quotes from the texts is clear evidence for her happy mind.

Nadezhda cleaned the apartment, then took a bath, applied a yeast facial mask, and went to bed earlier than usual. Even before she had time to think about what she was going to wear in the evening she'd fallen asleep. The next day she arose refreshed and walked a part of the way with pleasure. All day long she heard Solvejg's words ringing in her head: "And you'll return to me, my heart tells me, my heart tells me..." she tried to stifle this singing with self-mockery, though, for that was really going too far.

In the evening when she was getting ready to go for the shopping she got Natasha's phone call. Natasha wanted her to come and to stay with her. Usually she didn't have the habit of phoning her mother and enquiring her news. But when she was in need she phoned her mother and said:

"It would be great if you could spend the night. Seriozha would be late again. The baby was crying a lot-it was probably her teeth. The wind was so strong it was blowing right through the windows. It was cold and very bleak. And mom would you please buy some fruits? There was none here. And one more favour-would you get some two-kopek pieces for the phone?"

Thus it becomes clear that Natasha was very selfish. She was a daughter who wants her mother only when she was in need, ie; when nobody was there to help her.

Nadezhda Mikhailovna on the other hand disliked disappointing her daughter, but her mind wishes to receive Viktor. While doing the shopping to receive Viktor she brought some apples and grapes for Natasha. From her act we can infer that even though Nadezhda was in a hurry to receive Viktor in her mind she always gave preference to her daughter. After her marriage Natasha never showed any attachment to her mother. She only called her when she was in need. But Nadezhda never showed any indifference in behaviour to Natasha. A true mother never hates her children. She always supports and loves her children and will be ready to sacrifice her happiness for the well-being of her children. Here we can see after making all the arrangements to receive Viktor at the very last moment her mind changed and she goes to her daughter.

So Nadezhda was a mother who sacrificed her whole life for the happiness of her only daughter. As a wife she failed to get the love and care of her husband and at the end when she got acquainted with a young man, for the sake of her daughter she decided to avoid him. In all the way we can conclude that Nadezhda was an unlucky wife and mother.

In Kamala Das' *The Cruel Ring of Truth* we can find the similar type of a widowed mother. Her husband had died the year the daughter was born. Since then she had lived her life trying hard to fulfil the obligations of both father and mother. As a woman she also had all sorts of emotions and feelings. But she suppressed all her emotions and lived for her daughter. She feared that a second marriage would badly affect her daughter's future life. Many men had tried to tempt her into sin in the days when her beauty was a burden to her in the absence of a husband. But she had lived, envisioning both god and goddess in her daughter, without walking into anyone's sexual snares.

The mother loved and cared her daughter very much. To conceal from her daughter her middle-class origins, she had borrowed money from her friends, bought her silk clothes, arranged the top teachers of the city for her tuition, and lit coloured bulbs on the branches of trees in the garden on her birthdays. She brought up her without let her know any hardships in life. So the daughter never had any difficulties in her life.

The daughter was in love with another youth before marriage. He was an engineer in the Navy. That relationship was shattered because of some misunderstanding. The daughter was responsible for the way the relationship crashed. But the mother didn't feel like rebuking her. She was always ready to find excuses for her daughter's actions and to put courage into her. On account of this, perhaps, her daughter embraced her on many occasions and whispered in her ear: "My mother is the best mother in the world". All these moments the mother used to feel in her underbelly a pain born of pride. She viewed as enemies the friends who advised her to restrain her daughter. In those days she needed only her daughter's love.

From this it is clear that due to her excessive love the mother always supported her daughter without even thinking whether her daughter's actions were right or wrong. Eventually the mother had given her in marriage to a rich, well-behaved youth. She told her neighbours countless times that, through that marriage, she had got a son as well. But the mother started eating the bitter fruits of loneliness for the first time in her life when her married daughter grew gradually distant from her. She had been too busy observing how her daughter moved about and how her facial expressions changed. The son-in-law hadn't spoken to her even formally after the wedding. Her daughter shrugged her shoulders when she asked her who was responsible for her son-in-laws coldness towards her.

Till her marriage the daughter showed affection to her mother because her mother fulfilled all her desires and supported her in all her problems. But this daughter changed a lot after the marriage. The sudden change in the daughter's behaviour mentally depressed the mother. Before her daughter's marriage when she lay at night waiting for sleep with her arms around her daughter, she had never thought in her wildest dreams that days without her daughter and without her love were in store for her. Her conviction was that she would live with her daughter till death. But the very next day after the daughter's marriage she grew distant from her.

When the mother went to her daughter's house the behaviour of her only daughter gave her great pain. The daughter's harsh behaviour to the mother can be clear from her words:

"Why did you come so early, ma?" she asked.

The mother had thought that seeing her, she would be happy and kiss her on the cheeks as she used to. But there were no demonstrations of love.

"How come this change?" asked the mother.

"Change? What change?" asked the daughter.

"You don't seem to be happy I came. The bananas and vegetables I've brought you are in the car shed. Ask the servant to take them to the kitchen", said the mother.

"Mother, don't bring vegetables any more", said the daughter. "He doesn't like it".

"You don't use vegetables?"

The daughter was silent.

"What have I done, child?" asked the mother. "Why do you both of you treat me so cruelly or are you taken in somebody's cooked up stories?"

The daughter was silent at that moment too. The mother drove back, without waiting even to have tea. She realised that her presence was distasteful, not to the son-in-law alone, but to her daughter as well.

From the daughter's words we can understand that the daughter hated seeing her mother and talking with her. The mother went to see her daughter with lots of expectations. But she can't endure the daughter's behaviour and drove back. That day the mother did not have her bath or cook her food. She sobbed, lying flat on her back in the darkened room and recalling over and over episodes from her daughter's childhood. She realised that her daughter's bits of conversation and mannerisms which used to delight her in the past were now making her very sad. She was surprised how her loving daughter has changed suddenly and become so cruel to her. She can't endure her loneliness.

With the passage of time the mother grew absolutely lonely. Her hair turned quite grey. She lost her sleep and always thought about her daughter. Her blood pressure went up due to lack of sleep, and her neighbours could view her only with sympathy. The daughter never came to see her and not even phoned her. Though her daughter never came to see her she never hates her. That's why when the neighbours asked her whether her daughter visits her she told them that she comes at night because both of them were busy during the day. Thus she learnt even to utter lies for her daughter. She told like this because she disliked others abusing her daughter.

When the mother was hospitalised she told her neighbour bystanders not to frighten her daughter unnecessarily by informing her that she was hospitalised. The mother told like this because she knew that her daughter will not come to see her and she didn't like others abusing her daughter. From this conversation it becomes clear that a true mother can't hate her children even though they didn't loved her back.

"Didn't your daughter come?" asked the launderer. She gave a tired smile. "She doesn't know", she said.

"I told her", said the greengrocer. "I went there this morning and told them. Master said they'd come to the hospital with money".

"It's getting dark", said the launderer.

"They may not be coming now", said the sweeper.

"Which scandalmonger has lied to the son about the mother? Sinner! Not even two years have passed after the daughter's wedding. She's so withered", the greengrocer said.

"This may be the work of your own daughter", said the sweeper. "She may have thought he should not hear from mother's lips the incidents of the past".

The mother was shocked at those words. But she could hear in them the cruel ring of truth. Because there was no other reason for her daughter's rude behaviour. She might have frightened that if her husband mingled with her mother sometimes she might tell him about her past love affair. So in order to make her life secure she grew distant from her mother and also turned her husband against her mother. To make her life secure and happy the daughter knowingly avoids her mother. So here the daughter is too cruel to her mother, the only person who had suffered all alone to bring up her after her father's death. So here the mother's mind was utterly collapsed when she came to know that her only daughter and son-in-law have no attachment to her.

Natalya Baranskaya's another story named *Lubka* is also about a widowed mother and her daughter. Lubka's mother Paraskova Egorovna Sapozhnikova was a soldier's widow. Lubka was her only daughter. The war had taken Paraskovya's husband away. She had married Ivan for love when she was only twenty-two. Two months later, before they'd managed to start a child, the war came and Ivan left. Praskovya received letters from Ivan until 1944. Then the letters stopped. She waited as the months passed. She cried, lost weight, ran to the army offices to get news. But they could tell her nothing; it seemed that they themselves knew nothing.

Praskovya received news of her husband's death on the eve of Victory Day, in April 1945. She did not shriek or scream. But all joy left her, her feelings were numbed. On Victory Day she looked herself in her room and wouldn't come out. Nobody could make her. They were frightened she might harm herself.

When Praskovya come out she seemed greatly changed. She began going out in a crowd, drinking and singing. She got involved with other men, got through three, that summer alone. But everything was passing fancy; nothing was serious, as if she was acting out of spite. Her heart was sad and her body wanted fun. That's why she went with other men. Praskovya's socialising had a desperate quality; she began to drink heavily and have affairs shamelessly. In 1949 Praskovya became pregnant. She thought the father was the captain. She'd liked him best of all, he was nice-looking and affectionate, and he'd stayed with her for ten whole days. The baby was a girl. Praskovya registered her patronymic as 'Ivan' after her husband because, no matter who the father of the baby was, her husband had been 'Ivan'.

Praskovya's daughter caused her a lot of trouble. The visitors no longer stayed with her, they felt uneasy there. She had to live in her wages alone, and they didn't amount to much. They didn't look after the babies' very well in the crèche and little Lubka was often ill. She was even in hospital twice. And she recovered slowly. She was a weak child. Praskovya suffered with her and got thin and lost her looks. She no longer had any time for men; she didn't need them anymore and so Praskovya had remained alone. She had nobody. Lubka was her whole joy. She thought: "oh that terrible war – it took your father away from us, and how can I bring up a child without its father? Oh, bitter fate…"

Through Praskovya's mind Baranskaya had shown the lament of a poor widow struggling to bring up a child.

Later Praskovya get a job in the food trade. She got on well in the restaurant kitchen. She worked well and quickly she coped with everything. Thus, as a widowed mother Praskovya had undergone a lot of troubles to bring up Lubka.

Lubka grew up in freedom and blossomed like a flower. When Lubka started going school Praskovya again became aware of her loneliness. She wanted to get married to a respectable man so that Lubka would have a good father. But no one married her and she and Lubka lived alone. Lubka never get a proper guidance from her mother. When she said that she was not interested in going to school her mother didn't compel her to go. Normally if the children fall behind they can be helped. But when Lubka out of childish stupidity, left school, her mother didn't do anything. If her mother might have moved her to another school, she might have completed her school education.

When Lubka entered into her youth she had lot of friends and she and her friends became nuisance to the other people in her flat. In the Comrades court most of the tenants was of the opinion to remove Lubka from their housing authority area and transfer her to another more remote part of the Soviet Union. Hearing this for the first time in her life Lubka felt afraid because she couldn't go anywhere. She couldn't leave her mother. It was her mother who undresses her and put her to bed each night. So Lubka could not abandon her mother. In the comrade's court when her neighbours cursed and laughed at her mother it hurt Lubka deeply and made her very sad. Praskovya wasn't really bad. She'd never hurt or punished her. Praskovya was also plunged into panic. She thought" they couldn't send my little Lubka away. What could she do? Where could she go? Where could she get help? She was quite inexperienced in these matters, but I knew that I can't live without

Lubka. I had no one, not a living soul, except Lubka".

From Praskovya's thought it is true that she loved her daughter passionately. She had known that this was a love given her for her whole life, until death itself. Even though she brought up Lubka with great difficulty she never brought up her in the right way. That was why Lubka got mixed up with bad friends and became nuisance to her neighbours. If Praskovya had forbidden her from mingling with bad friends the comrade's court would not have interfered in their personal life. Lubka thought about the situation of her life only when the comrade's court gave warning to her. Thus the main reason for Lubka's ruin was that she failed to get good upbringing.

At the end we can find that Lubka decided to lead a good life avoiding her bad friends. The reason behind her change was a true love affair. When Mikhail the young man working with her in her factory promised to marry her, a sudden change appeared in her behaviour. So the feeling that someone was there to love her made a complete change in her life.

Kamala Das' story *The Mother and Son (Ammayum Makanum)* tells the story of a middle-aged woman who lived almost a lonely life with her son and who no longer cared for her. Unni started hating his mother when he was fifteen year old. His father was in Qatar and he and his mother were alone at home. In his childhood days Unni liked his mother very much and he shared everything with his mother. But later he started avoiding his mother. His mother on the other hand always tried to establish a friendship with Unni.

Unni thought that his mother's way of talking and her style of pronunciation would destroy his dignity before others. Because of this he always avoided her getting acquainted with his friends and he didn't take her to his school for the anniversary. Unnis's disgust in taking her can be clear from these words:

"Nobody's mother is coming, so you also don't come for the anniversary" Unni said.

Mother became sad and said, "I want to see your programme"

"How many times I have presented before you the programme and why are you persuading me to take you to School. If you come I will stay hear saying that I have fever. I will not go for the anniversary".

Unni wanted his mother to behave like a modern lady. His friend's mothers were all modern. They had servants in their houses and they used to read books and even went for film in the day time. But his mother alone was always busy with cleaning, washing and other household duties. Such manners of his mother made him more disgust. When he told her to appoint a servant she said that if she appoints a servant she would have no task to do and by simply sitting she would be bed-ridden. Hearing her words Unni thought that it was better to introduce the bed-ridden mother in front of others than this typical one.

From Unni's thought we can assume that because of the excessive infatuation to modernization, Unni started to avoid her. The sudden change in his behaviour may be due to the problems of teenage. Though Unni behaved rudely to her she never hated him or scolded him. From this conversation we can understand how much he cared her son:

"Mother, did you wish to live with father in Qatar. Hearing this mother said "how can I go to Qatar leaving you alone here? Who will prepare food for you if I am not here?"

"You won't bother about me. I will have food from the hotel. You must live happily without doing any work".

"How can I live happily there without seeing you?"

"The food you prepare are not having any taste. Now on wards you don't make food. Give me money. I will go to Bimbees and have food".

Hearing this she felt very sad and begged him "I will make you any food which you like. Please don't take food from the hotel and make your stomach upset".

Unni's mother never liked to become a burden to others. That's why she told Unni that she had no fascination to see Qatar. Father was sending enough money for them and she was not interested to go there and become a burden for him. After saying this, her eyes were filled with tears. From her tears we can infer that she knew that her husband also was not interested in her. So as a wife and also as a mother she failed to get the love which she expected from them.

An unexpected death takes Unni's mother from him. She died

in an accident. While she was crossing the road a bus knocked down her. Seeing her dead body Unni burst into tears. He can't endure her unexpected death. Thinking about his ruthless behaviour to her he felt regret. With great sorrow he bent respectfully at her feet. Unni's father was there from Qatar and he told the neighbours that after Unni's exam he will take him to Qatar. For the first time in his life Unni slept in his home without his mother. The separation of his mother was really intolerable to him. Unni went to Bimbees, had chicken and for the first time in his life he smoked. Then he said to himself "I killed my mother".

The son in this story is repenting thinking of his dead mother. His remorse takes the form of regret. He felt guilty for behaving rudely to his mother. Only after his mother's death he understands the value of his mother. Till then he hated his mother because she was an unstylish lady. He always compared his mother with his friend's mothers who were modern and he wanted his mother to become like that. He realised his mistake only after her death. He felt remorse thinking that he failed to give love to his mother.

In Natalya Baranskaya's *At her Father's and At her Mother's Place* we can find a daughter's frustrated mind whose father and mother were living separately. Natalya's father and mother started living separately when she was only five years old. She lived with her mother. When she was thirteen years old she starts out living at her dad's house, which was a carefree, happy, good life.

Talya liked her father very much. She enjoyed every minute she spent with him. He played with him and helped her in her studies. She thought how nice it was there with him and what a shame it was that they didn't all live together. Talya felt like this because at her mother's home she was always alone. Her mother was always busy and she never gets time to spend with her. So her father's behaviour gave her childish mind great pleasure. When her father presented her a watch Talya was shrieked with joy. She felt that much of joy because she and her mother were living alone and there was nobody there to give her gifts. So when her father presented her a watch she was overjoyed because in her life it was the first gift she was getting.

Their happy, carefree life came to an abrupt end when Talya found a note sent to her father from an admirer. The letter ended with many kisses and was signed 'Rita'. We can find that a feeling of utter weariness swept over Talya when she understands that her father has illegal relationship with a strange woman. That's why she went to her mother immediately. But she didn't tell anything about the letter to her father. Talya's behaviour shows that even though she was a small girl she had a mature state of mind. That's why without even telling about the letter to her father she decided to go back to her mother. She loved her father very much, but after reading the letter her mind had changed. She never expected such a thing from her father and she went back to her mother.

Talya's father's house was well-furnished and everything in the house looks neat and tidy. But her mother who was financially poorer than her father was always busy and she had no time to arrange things in the house or we can say that she was not interested in that kind of things.

After staying with her father for some days Talya had some changes. She thought why everything was so horrible at her home and she decided to clean her home. Talya was very much conscious about the poor condition of her house and the food they eat. Since she had a luxurious life with her father her mind wishes to lead such a life with her mother also.

Talya remembered a conversation that she had once, long ago, with her mother. "Why don't we use a tablecloth every day?" said Talya

"Is a table cloth important? Does your happiness depend on something like that?"

At that time Talya hadn't thought about her mother's words, she had just decided that because her mother was so seldom home she didn't care. But later she understands that her mother didn't like it because her dad was not living with them. She remembered another home, the sunny warm home of her early childhood. In that home everything was so perfect. Her mother arranged everything neatly and beautifully. So Talya understood that her father's absence made her mother so uneasy.

Talya's mother always went to work early in the morning, before Talya was properly awake. Though she was a nurse, she had a lot of other things to do as well, besides her work. Even in her off days she was busy. Talya knew about her mother's work. Talya didn't ask questions about her mother's visitors. It was obvious to her that people needed her mother and that was why her mother gave them all her time. She rarely arrived home before nine or ten in the evening, and then she would have to wash, sew and cook. In her life Talya never accused her mother. As a daughter she always supported her. Even though she went with her father and lived a luxurious life with him, she never forgets her mother. She loved her very much and was eager to see her. Talya's love to her mother can be clear from the following words:

"Mum, what's happened to you? I've missed you, but I can't wait any longer. I've to go to bed. Don't leave tomorrow without waking me first. A hundred kisses".

If Talya's mother had asked her what she wanted, Talya could have named a great many things without difficulty. But she never tormented her mother. She knew their condition and always adjusted to it. Her mother teaches her like that. Talya's mother was an ideal mother. She had brought up her daughter by making aware of her all the difficulties that the different classes of people suffering to sustain their life. By understanding these things Talya never showed any obstination to any matter. She always adjusted herself. Since she brought up Talya in the right way she shows more maturity than the children of her age. From the following words it is clear that Talya's mother was an ideal mother:

"Talya we can discuss our poverty some other time, but I would like to say something to you; in our country how many people have very hard live; they lack the most elementary necessities; they never get enough to eat. We must arrange our common lives so that everybody has a good life, do you understand? We Bolsheviks must think of ourselves last".

Talya didn't tell her mother anything about the letter she read from her father's home. This shows Talya's maturity. She knew that her mother will be tensed hearing about it. So Talya kept it as a secret. But she asked her mother why they were living separately. Talya asked her mother about their separation because she wanted to know whether her mother knew anything about the lady who wrote letter to her father or was there any other reason behind her father's and mother's separation. As a grown up daughter she has the right to know about it. While talking about that matter her eyes became cloudy with tears. This itself shows how distressed she was. There existed some reason behind their separation which only her mother and father know.

Talya's mother never accused her husband. She always told her daughter that he was a good man and Talya must love him. Though Talya's father and mother were living separately Talya's mother never hated her husband. Her true love to her husband is evident from her words to Talya:

"Talya, your father is a good man, do you hear? You must believe me, he's a fine man. He is a good man, and you must love him, you must".

If Talya had known the reason behind their separation she might not have tormented herself that much. But she didn't know anything. She was thinking about her mother and father. Both of them were good people. She loved them both, her father as well, in spite of the letter. From her mother's words it is clear that she still loved him very much. She saw her mother, her brisk step, her swift movements, her infectious, ringing laugh, and her eyes, always brilliant, always changing colour, from grey-blue to sky-blue. She thought unhappy people didn't have eyes like that and how could he have stopped loving her and what had happened between them. All these questions have no answers in Talya's mind.

Here, we come across the fact that children are always the victim of a broken family. Talya the young girl's mind was perplexed. She was very much confused. Seeing her friend's happy family she very much yearned to live together with her father and mother. If her father and mother were living together she can get rid off from her poor state of living. Because her father was financially high and thus her mother could have relief from all the struggles as done to bring up her. She wished for their reunion. She very much wanted to live together with her father and mother. That's why she enquired her mother why they were separated. But her mother was not ready to reveal it. So Talya's desire of leading a happy united family doesn't happen.

The Alienated Mothers: A Comparative Study of Nadezhda Mikhailovna, Praskovya Egorovna and Others

The mother's in the selected stories of both Natalya Baranskaya and Kamala Das were leading a lonely life. The mothers in Natalya Baranskaya's *The Kiss, Lubka* and Kamala Das' *The Cruel Ring of Truth* were widowed. The mother in Baranskaya's *At Her Father's and At Her Mother's Place* was leading a lonely life because she was divorced and the mother in Kamala Das' *Unni* was leading a lonely life because her husband was in Qatar.

The mental states of a widowed mother are shown in the stories of Natalya Baranskaya's *The Kiss* and Kamala Das' *The Cruel Ring of Truth.* Both the mothers became widows in their youth itself and they brought up their daughters all alone sacrificing all their happiness. Many men had tried to tempt them into sin but without walking into anyone's sexual snares they lived for their daughters. When they had given their daughters in marriage to rich, well-behaved youth they believed that their daughters and sons-in-law would be there with them till the last breath. But unexpectedly, after the daughter's marriage when they began to behave like a stranger, the mother's beliefs get collapsed.

The mother Nadezhda Mikhailovna in Baranskaya's story *The Kiss* got acquainted with Viktor a young man in order to get out of her loneliness. But her obligation towards her daughter forced her to avoid him. She always gave more importance to her daughter's feelings even though her daughter never showed any attachment to her after marriage.

Both these mothers had no other blood relations to share their feelings. Nobody was there to help them. In their life they never enjoyed any sort of happiness. They had sacrificed their whole life for the well-being of their daughters. But the selfish daughters never cared their mother. Hence, the mother in these stories is really an embodiment of tolerance.

The mother named Praskovya Egorovna in Baranskaya's story *Lubka* was also a widow. She had lived with her husband only two months after their marriage. Her husband's life was lost in a war. She was just twenty-two years at the time of his death. We can notice that in one thing Praskovya was different from the above discussed mothers. The mothers in Baranskaya's *The Kiss* ad Kamala Das' *The Cruel Ring of Truth* never indulge in extra-martial relations. But Praskovya had illegal relationship with many men after her husband's death and she became pregnant only one year after her husband's death. She was not sure about her daughter Lubka's father since she had relationship with many men.

Praskovya was not aware of bringing up children in the right way. She didn't give much care to Lubka's studies and her behaviours. When Lubka said that she was not interested in going to school Praskovya never compelled her to go to school. Hence Lubka stopped her studies at the age of fourteen and she went to work in the factory. Lubka had a lot of friends and she and her friends became a nuisance to their neighbours. If Praskovya had given proper guidance Lubka's life would not have been spoiled. She would get good education and would be able to make out right and wrong. But throughout her life she was always careless in nature. She became a widow at the very first days of her marital life. She loved Lubka very much though she was a failure in giving proper guidance to Lubka. She alone brought up Lubka. Praskovya was very hard working and in her tormenting life she gets very little joy.

The mother in Baranskaya's story *At Her Fathers and At Her Mothers Place,* even though leading a lonely life due to some personal problems with her husband brought up her daughter in the right way. Their only daughter Talya was thirteen years old and they were separated when Talya was only five years old. After that she who was a nurse brought up her daughter without asking any help from her husband who was a doctor.

She was an ideal mother. She brought up her daughter by making her aware of the difficulties faced by the common people. Thus Talya always behaved like a matured girl. She was aware of their living condition and always adjusted to it and never tormented her mother.

Here, though her husband was alive, Talya's mother was living as a widow, because they were living separated for eight years. But she never accused her husband for their separation. Only she and her husband know the reason behind their separation. She not even told it to her only daughter. She always tells her that her father was a nice man and she must love him. So in all the way Talya's mother was an ideal wife and an ideal mother.

The mother in Kamala Das' *The Mother and Son* was also living as a widow since her husband was in Qatar. Her husband who was in Qatar never showed any interest in her. Every month he sends enough money to her but she fails to get the love which she wishes to get from a husband. Her only son was also not giving her much care and love which she desired to get. Unni was always tried to isolate her. He was ashamed to introduce his mother to his friends because she was an unstylish lady and his friend's mothers were modern. She was in great grief because of his rude behaviour.

Even though she failed to get the love and care from her son and husband she never hated them, instead she loved them and in her life she always gave more preference to them. But she died unexpectedly in an accident and only after her death Unni understands the value of his mother. So here we can find a mother who died unexpectedly without getting the love and care which she wishes to get from his son and husband.

So by analyzing the mother characters of Natalya Baranskaya and Kamala Das we attain a universal truth that the mothers in the whole world are alike. Beyond the culture and nation every mothers are alike. Though their children never showed any love towards them they always loved them and were not able to hate them. They were ready to sacrifice all their joys for the well being of their children. These mothers are embodiments of selfless love.

12
REAL WOMEN IN THE SHORT STORIES OF NATALYA BARANSKAYA AND KAMALA DAS

Women's writing is a transparent expression of their authentic experience. The myriad conflicts faced by women in their daily lives are woven into a fictional or a real world. Short stories written by women writers have the aim of creating an urgent awareness amongst people regarding the position of women in the society and also the injustice done to them. They deal with social inequalities and prevalent exploitations.

The study of Natalya Baranskaya and Kamala Das reveals that these authors reconstruct the life of Russian and Indian women and particularly their suppression and social reaction through their stories. Their short fictions depict the agony of woman and her social oppression. In their works Natalya Baranskaya and Kamala Das depict the inner world of modern women with great psychological insight and questions with great vehemence. Both the writers reveal their vision and philosophy of life through their short fictions.

In Russia the glasnost marked a veritable bloom in women's culture. In the 1970s a new generation of women writers come to public attention. Natalya Baranskaya belonged to this group. Natalya Baranskaya's stories internally, concentrate on the nuclear family and its problems, on personal relationships. The short fictions of Natalya Baranskaya have shown new heroines – the "real woman" who faces difficulties in everyday life. Her works concentrate on the middle class, chiefly the urban technical intelligentsia. Selfishness and alienation govern the relations between family members, spouses, lovers and friends. Natalya Baranskaya lovingly dwells upon woman as mother and child-bearer. She pinpoints the defects of society, she wishes things to change, but she does not advocate rupture in family or society.

In India the short text had always been popular in the regional languages among women writers. Kerala, can boast of a long line of women short story writers in Malayalam. Kamala Das is equally at home both in the regional language as well as in English. She is accepted as an Indian English poet and as a Malayalam short story writer. She has written over a hundred and fifty stories in Malayalam, but has used the short story from very sparingly in English. She is a writer who consistently dwells deep into her consciousness to create female images that are at once herself and the other. Her stories are a reproduction of the lives of women characters caught in different moods and situations. Human relationship is the theme of a large number of the stories, especially, relationship between man and woman. The harmonies and discords, the ecstasies and agonies of marital as well as extra-marital love are portrayed in her stories.

While analysing the familial relations in India and Russia in the short fictions of Natalya Baranskaya and Kamala Das many similarities are found even though the cultural, social and economic conditions are different in both countries. The traditional family of the past has undergone tremendous changes in both countries. One can easily understand the social life of Russia and India through the works of Natalya Baranskaya and Kamala Das. Images of familial relationships depicted in their prose works help to analyse the patterns of family existing in these countries. These patterns vary according to the cultural and social background of the people belonging to various social strata in both countries.

The family is a functional unit which connects man to the external world. It is the locus of woman's power. Overtones of disintegration, power, struggle and alienation have adversely affected the structure of the family. Natalya Baranskaya and Kamala Das examined their characters against the backdrop of family.

The most common theme in fiction is human relationship particularly the man-woman relationship. Nowadays this theme becomes more important due to rapid industrialization, growing awareness among women of their rights and individualism and the westernization of attitudes and lives of the people. Natalya Baranskaya and Kamala Das treat this subject in a different manner from that of earlier fiction writers. They portray the relationships between man and woman as it is, whereas earlier novelists concentrated on as it should be. Most of their female protagonists are alienated from the world, from society, from families, from parents and even from their own selves because they are not ordinary people but individuals. Tensions, worries, depression, disappointments, anxiety and fear became their lot and they lose their sense of sanity and mental poise. Baranskaya's character Olga, Kamala Das' characters Subhadra and Sheela are characterised by loneliness and lack of communication with their family. The social expectations of the wife or her incompatibility are sources of conflict in husband-wife relationship. The patriarchal set up of the family accentuates these conflicts.

By analysing the select fictions of Natalaya Baranskaya and Kamala Das we find that family and familial relationships occupy important parts in their fictional world. But the remarkable thing is that more often the familial relationships are not harmonious. We cannot find a single family in any of their works which can be called completely perfect. Natalaya Baranskaya and Kamala Das portray real life situations in their stories. Both these writers purpose is to see their women characters as human with their weakness and potentialities which are indeed caught in the web of their own compulsions. Their stories have been examined as the manifesto of female predicament and creative release of the feminine sensibility. Their feminism is not anti-male and their women characters need man's loving company and aspire for the bliss and thrill of life which are ever denied to them.

Natalya Baranskaya and Kamala Das look at the predicament of women and visualise life for a woman as a series of obligations and commitments. In addition to the existentialistic reality of life they evoke sentiment and sensibility of women for their role and respect in society. They closely examined the emotional world of womankind. Both Natalya Baranskaya and Kamala Das have natural preference for writing about women characters. They portray women as not totally cut off from familial and social ties but women who remain within these orbits and protest against monotony, injustice and humiliation.

Although Natalya Baranskaya and Kamala Das are pre-occupied with the theme of incompatible marital couples yet we come across different kinds of women characters like lonely mothers in their stories. Both the writers predominantly centre their attention of the isolation and struggles associated with maternity, there by challenging its exalted status within Russian and Indian culture. Their portrayal of the loneliness of the mothers and their essential need for affection and companionship is notable in the stories Baranskaya's *The Kiss* and Kamala Das' *The Cruel Ring of Truth,* when their daughters gave little care to them after their marriage. By analyzing the mother characters of Natalya Baranskaya and Kamala Das we attain a universal truth that the mothers in the whole world are alike. Beyond the culture and nation every mothers are alike. They are embodiments of selfless love for their wards. Though their children never showed any love towards them they always loved them and were not able to hate them. They were ready to sacrifice all their joys for the well being of their children.

Natalya Baranskaya and Kamala Das can be considered doyens of female fiction in their respective literatures. The publication of Baranskaya's *A Week Like Any Other* caused great sensation mainly because of its sociological value. Baranskaya herself mentions that there had been nothing written, either fiction or fact, about how hard life was for women, who legally have equal rights with men. In the same way Kamala Das' *My Story* created great sensation as it spoke unabashedly about women's sexual desires, thereby giving a new dimension to the Malayalam short stories.

Although Baranskaya broaches the issue of gender inequality she handles it mildly and carefully. She had no feminist intention to oppose the Soviet system. She even tries to glorify love, whether it be love of mother to her daughter, or love towards another man and husband. Kamala Das on the other hand tries to expose the hypocrisies of a society living in an illusionary world of pseudo morality and oblivious of the stark realities around. She moves a step forward in the portrayal of unique sexual intimacy between heroines and thereby quashing the conventional values of man-woman relationships.

BIBLIOGRAPHY

Abrams, M.H., and Geoffrey Gatt Harpham, *A Glossary of Literary Terms*; Cengage Learning, Delhi, 2012.

Adele Marie Barker (ed.), *A History of Women's Writing in Russia*, Cambridge University Press, 2002.

Adele Marie Barker and Jehanne M Gheith (ed.) A History of Women's writing in Russia, Cambridge University Press, 2004.

Andrew, Joe, *Russian writes and Society in the second half of the nineteenth century,* The Mac Millan Press Ltd., London, 1982.

Asha Chaubey (Dr.) Women on Women: Indian & Women Writers Perspectives on Woman, Aadi Publications, Jaipur, 2011.

Auty, Robert Oblonsky, Dimitry (Ed). *An Introduction to Russian History*; Cambridge University Press, 1991.

Benn, Anna and Bartlett, Rosamund; Literary Russia, A Guide; Papermac, London, 1997.

Beth Holmgren, *Women's Works in Stalin's time*, Indiana University Press, 1993.

Books, Peter. Psychonalysis and Story Telling. Oxford: Blackwell, 1994.

Chaithanya, Krishna, *A History of Malayalam Literature*, Orient Longman: Bombay, 1995.

Clara Nubile, The Danger of Gender, Caste Class and Gender in Contemporary Indian Women's Writing; Sarup & Sons,

New Delhi, 2003.

Das Kamala, *Ente Katha*. Kottayam: DC Books, 1998.

Das Kamala, *My Story*; Harper Collins Publishers; New Delhi, 2009.

Das Kamala, *Neermathalam Pootha Kalam*, Kottyam: DC Books, 1993.

Das Kamala, *Padmavathi, the Harlot and Other Stories*, New Delhi: Sterling Publishers, 1992.

Das, Kamala, *The Sandal Trees and Other Stories*. Hyderabad: Disha Books, Orient Longman Ltd., 1995.

Dwivedi, A.N., Kamala Das and Her Poetry; Atlantic Publishers and Distributors, New Delhi, 2006.

Gopalakrishnan, P.K., The Cultural History of Kerala (Mal.). Trivandrum, Kerala Bhasha Institute, 1974.

Graham Stephenson, History of Russia, 1812-1945. MacMillan & Co., Ltd., 1969.

Hetena Goscilo (ed.) Balancing acts, Dell Publishers, New York, 1991.

Hudson, William Henri, An Introduction to the Study of Literature; Kalyani Publishers, New Delhi, 1982.

Inner Spaces, New Writing by Women from Kerala, Kali for Women B1/8 Hauskhas, New Delhi, 110016, 1993.

Iqbal Kaur (ed.) Prespectives on Kamala Das's Prose, Intellectual Publishing House, New Delhi, 1995.

Iyengar, K.R. Srinivasa. *Indian Writing in English*. New Delhi: Sterling, 1994.

Jain, Jazhir (ed.) *Women's Writing*. Jaipur: Rawat, 1996.

Jasbir Jain, Women's Writing, Text and Content, Rawat Publications, Jaipur and New Delhi, 2004.

Johar, D. Image of Women, Shiva Publishers, Udaipur, 1995.

Krishna Swamy, Shantha. *The woman in Indian fiction in English*. New Delhi: Ashish, 1983.

Kumar, Gajendra, *"Indian English Literature – A New Perspective*. New Delhi: Sarup, 2001.

Madhavikutty, *Balyakalasmaranakal*. Kottayam: DC Books, 1987.

Madhavikutty, *Diarikkuripukal*. Kottayam: DC Books, 2004.

Madhavikutty, *Madhavikuttiyude Kathakal Sampoornam 2nd ed*. Kottayam: DC Books, 2004.

Madhavikutty, *Madhavikuttiyude Kathakal*. 10th ed. Kottayam: DC Books, 2003.

Madhavikutty, *Madhavikuttiyude Premakathakal 2nd ed*. Calicut: Olive Publications Pvt. Ltd. 1999.

Madhavikutty, *Madhavikuttiyude Sthreekal*, Kozhikode: Mathrubhoomi Books, 2004.

Madhra, S.M., The position of Women in Indian life. New Delhi, Neeraj Publishing House, 1981.

Marina Ledkovsky, *Dictionary of Russian Women Writers*, Praeger, 1994.

Masha Gessen (ed.) *Half a Revolution*, Cleis, New York, 1995.

Meena Kelka & Deepti Gangavane, *Feminism in Search of an Identity, The Indian Context*, Rawat Publications, Jaipur and New Delhi, 2003.

Mirsky, D.S. *A History of Russian Literature*; Routledge, and Kegan Paul: London, 1968.

Moser, Charles, A. (Ed.) *The Cambridge History of Russian Literature*, Cambridge University Press, 1996.

Nair, Sreediv K., "Kamala Das – Excerpis from An Interview Samyukta. A journal of women's studies. Vol.1, No.1 Jan. 2001.

Nataly a Baranskaya. *A week like Any Other*. Novellas and Stories; Seal Press, 1990.

Neeru Tandon, Anita Desai and Her Fictional World; Atlantic Publishers, New Delhi, 2008.

Neil Cornwell (ed.) *Russian Literature,* Routledge: London, 2001.

Nirmala S. (ed.) Faces: *Women's Resonances in World Literatures*, Department of Russian, Calicut University, 2008.

Pirumova, N., Itenberg. B. & Antonov, V., *Russia and the West 19th century*; Progress Publishers: Moscow, 1990.

Prasantha Kumar, N. *Writing the Female, A study of Kamala Das*, Bharatiya Sahitya Pratishthan, Kochi, 1998.

Ramanan, Mohan & Sailaja. P., *English and the Indian Short Story*; Orient Longman, New Delhi, 200.

Rosalind Marsh (ed.) *Gender and Russian Literature: New Perspectives*, Cambridge University Press, 1996.

Rzhersky, Nicholas, (Ed.), *An Anthology of Russian Literature*; M.E. Sharpe, London, 1996.

Rzhevsky, Nicholas, (Ed.), *The Cambridge Companion to Modern Russian Culture*; Cambridge University Press, 1998.

Sai Chandra Mouli, T. Charisma of Kamala Das, GNOSIS, New Delhi, 2010.

Seema Suneel, Man-Woman Relationship in Indian Fiction, Prestige Books, New Delhi, 1995.

Sree Sathupati Prasanna (ed.) *Indian Women Writing in English*: New Perspectives, New Delhi: Sarup & Sons, 2005.

Tharu, Susie K., Lalitha, (eds.) *Women's Writing in India: 600 BC to the Present*, Delhi: Oxford UP, 1995.

Usha Band, Atma Ram, *Woman in Indian Short Stories Feminist Perspective*; Rawat Publications, Jaipur & New Delhi, 2003.